SAVAGE HEARTS

LILI VALENTE

SAVAGE HEARTS

Rebel Hearts
Book Two

By Lili Valente

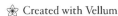 Created with Vellum

ABOUT THE BOOK

A year ago, four men slipped through the cracks in the criminal justice system.

They should be rotting behind bars. Instead they're spending Spring Break at a Costa Rican resort.

Well, you know what they say—Eat, drink, and merry boys, for tomorrow...you die.

With Samantha gone, I literally have nothing left to lose.

All that's left to do is pull the trigger...

And then I see her walking across the crowded airport—Sam, *my* Sam—and know she's here for the same reason I am.

For justice.

For revenge.

To take back everything that's been stolen from us.

We're both ready to walk through hell all over again.

But this time, we're coming out together.

Savage Hearts should be read after Rebel Hearts.
Savage Hearts was previously published as Fight for You. It has been retitled and recovered for this new edition.

Keep in touch with Lili...
Free book when you join Lili's newsletter
Friend Lili
Like Lili
Follow Lili on Bookbub
Follow Lili on Instagram

CHAPTER ONE

Sam

*"We do not have to visit a madhouse
to find disordered minds;
our planet is the mental
institution of the universe."*
-Goethe

The past never leaves us.

The past is a part of who we are, as much as our skin and bone and the lies we've told that we can never take back.

The choices we've made and the things we've suffered take every step with us, always present though not always seen.

. . .

*M*y dad is a geologist by profession, but an all-around science nerd for the love of a good mystery. When I was little, our family would spend our weekends exploring hidden island beaches, hiking up mist-shrouded mountains, or pawing through the volcanic soil atop Maui's dormant volcano.

On every trip, Dad's voice was the soundtrack for adventure. Before the divorce, Mom used to joke that she felt like she was living in a nature documentary. I could tell Dad's constant chatter annoyed her sometimes, but to me the stories he told were reason for wonder. It made me realize the world was full of mystery.

Every plant or animal we passed on a trail had a secret story to tell, an entire hidden world waiting to unfold to those who took the time to stop, observe, and ask the right questions.

It was Dad who taught me that palm trees aren't really trees at all. They're more closely related to the grass family and don't generate new cells the way trees do. Cut through an oak's bark and you'll see growth rings that tell the story of each year of the tree's life. Cut into a palm's trunk and you'll just leave a gash in the thick, spongy material of the plant.

And unlike the oak, whose yearly ring growth will eventually heal over the cut, protecting the plant from disease, the palm tree will bear an open wound for the rest of its life. Every insect and dangerous bacteria that floats by on an island breeze will be able to burrow straight into the heart of the palm and start devouring the plant from the inside out.

As I grew up, I started to think that people were a lot like both plants.

Sometimes, we're like an oak, growing past an old hurt, burying it under layers of new growth, moving forward and getting stronger despite the scar buried beneath the healthy outer shell. But sometimes, our wounds refuse to heal. Sometimes, they stay open and ugly, reminding us every time we look in the mirror that we will never be the same.

The hurt was too big, the cut too deep.

We will never move past it.

From this day, until our last day, the wound will make us an easy target, a weakened animal falling behind the rest of the herd, waiting for another predator to step in and finish the job the first one started.

*A*s I stumble down the courthouse steps, clinging to my dad's arm with my head tucked to my chin, ignoring the questions the reporters shout from either side of me as we press through the crowd, I wonder what the cameras see.

Do they see the hardened, selfish, sexually deviant monster the defense attorney made me out to be? Or do they see the stinging, screaming gash four boys cut through the middle of my heart?

Not guilty.

They were all found *not* guilty.

At the end of the day, the jury believed that I invited four boys to take turns with me, not that I fought and bled and cried. They believed that I spread rumors about Deidre to keep news of my sexual adventures from my boyfriend, not because I was traumatized after being raped.

As far as the law and the world at large are now concerned, Todd, Jeremy, J.D., and Scott are innocent and the rape never happened.

But *it did*.

It *did* and now I don't know what to do. How do I move on when I've been told the reason for my grief doesn't exist, and that my voice, my truth, means less than nothing?

Someone shouts my name.

I flinch and look up before I remember that I'm supposed to keep my gaze down until I get to the car waiting by the curb.

"How did you feel when you heard the verdict, Samantha?" The man in the suit shoving a microphone in my face has sweat beading on his upper lip. I stare at it for a moment, feeling ill, while my father springs to my defense.

"No comment," he growls, his arm tightening around me.

Sweaty Upper Lip says something else, but I can't make sense of it. My focus has shifted, homing in on Todd and his father, standing in the shade of the coral trees planted along the sidewalk.

Once I've spotted them, I can't seem to pull my gaze away.

Todd's father is shaking hands with a pretty, stick-thin reporter and smiling. Todd is nodding earnestly, his blue eyes wide with gratitude and his shaggy blond hair waving in the gentle breeze. He is the picture of innocence, proving he's a far better actor than his B-list celebrity father. If I didn't know he was a liar and a monster, I might be tempted to believe him, too.

But I was there the night Todd's human mask fell away and the devil beneath came out to play. I felt the cruelty in his touch. I heard him laugh while I cried and begged them to stop. I watched him smile as his friends took turns until the world was full of pain and blood ran down my thighs, mixed with the stickiness of other things I couldn't bear to think about.

And I remember the last words he shouted after me as I hobbled away from the pool table and ran, half-naked and sobbing, across the frat house's back lawn toward the quad.

You know you loved it, doll. Come back when you're ready for more.

Or maybe we'll come find you, Sammy.

The threat was the kill shot.

I had no idea how I would survive what they'd done once, let alone if they did it again. The terror the thought instilled, combined with the physical, mental, and emotional pain of the attack, swept through me like a hurricane, shattering the walls of the fortress protecting my most private, secret self.

And then J.D. put the video of what they'd done on the campus website and shoved the naked, innocent thing they'd exposed out into the driving rain.

It didn't matter that my face wasn't visible in the thirty seconds of footage or that it was only up on the site for a few hours before the administration shut it down. Everyone had already seen; everyone was already wondering who the girl might be. Hearing the hushed speculation in the library was like living through it all over again. I started to fear that it would never be over, that I would keep living through it, over and over again, every day until the day I died.

I spent January in hell, ravaged by rage, fear, and shame, forced to pretend everything was okay while I waited to find out if I was pregnant or if the test I'd taken at a local clinic would come back positive for HIV.

I don't remember telling my gossipy roommate that I'd heard it was Deidre Jones in the video. I don't remember going to classes or getting up for my morning run or exactly what I said to my stepbrother, Alec, the one time I worked up the courage to ask him why he hadn't stopped them.

Why he hadn't saved me.

But I remember the day I learned that Deidre had hung herself in her dorm room with crystal clarity, right down to the jeans I was wearing and the pattern of the coffee grounds floating in my cup when I heard the news. It was the day that everything changed, the day I began to hate myself as much as I hated the boys who had broken me.

By the time I took the stand in a packed Los Angeles courtroom, I thought I knew hate inside and out. I thought I understood it in a way I had understood very few things in my twenty years of life.

But I was wrong.

Todd's gaze meets mine across the crowded court-house steps and an ugly grin curves his full lips, and at that moment, I realize that hate is fathomless.

There is no end to it. I could sink down, down, down through the inky depths of my hatred for Todd Winslow for years and never reach the bottom. I could drink and eat nothing but hate and never be filled. And I could spend the rest of my life applying bandages to the wound he and his friends have ripped in my soul and it will never heal.

They say love and hate are opposite sides of the same coin, the two great transformative forces in the universe. One leads to light and freedom, the other feeds a fire that will consume you whole.

Anyone with sense would choose to be free.

I have parents who love me, believe me, and support me. I have a boyfriend who wants to be by my side, helping me pick up the pieces of my shattered life. The trial is over and I've spared Danny as much of the horror as I can. Now, all I have to do is pick up the phone. I know he will meet me on the island where we fell in love, hold me as long as I need to be held, and dedicate himself to loving me enough to make up for all the pain and injustice.

But I'm not sure there is enough love in the world for that. Enough love to make up for Todd's smile. Enough sand in the hourglass to make me forget that I went to the mat with evil and evil won.

But there might be enough hate.

Hate enough to make me strong, hate enough to turn a wound into a weapon.

I hold Todd's gaze, memorizing the exact curve of his lips, silently promising myself that one day, not too long from now, I will wipe that grin from his face. I will show him what it feels like to have every scrap of dignity, safety, and happiness stripped away and to be left twisting in the wind while the vultures swoop down to feed.

I'm silent in the car to the hotel my mother, father, and I have been staying at for the past few weeks. I stare out the window, ignoring my father's assurances that we'll appeal the court's decision, get a better lawyer, sue the bastards in civil court, do whatever it takes to make things right.

Things will never be right.

And I'm not going to beg for scraps of mercy or justice anymore.

I should have known better than to think a court and a bunch of anonymous jury members would take my vengeance for me. They don't understand. They can't see through my eyes, breathe my breath, or walk the dark, desolate halls in my soul that didn't exist before last New Year's Eve. No one can and no one ever will.

This is too personal, these crimes and the hatred they have left behind.

Violence creates a terrible intimacy between perpetrator and victim. For the past six months, I've rebelled against that intimacy, doing everything I could to distance myself from the pain and the boys who inflicted it. But now, I tear down the braces holding my feeble defenses in place. I close my eyes and let the memories sweep over me, drowning me in a flood of hurt, baptizing me in hatred and sealing it with a poisonous kiss.

By the time we arrive at the hotel, my decision is made.

I wait until my parents are distracted at the checkout counter, arguing with the clerk about whether we should be charged for the next two nights even though we're leaving early, and I step outside.

I walk calmly across the parking lot, get into my car, and pull out onto the highway. I head east and drive straight through the night, stopping only for gas and coffee. Around midnight, I turn off my ringer. Come sunrise, I chuck my phone out the window near the Texas state line.

I don't look into the rear view mirror or let regret creep into my heart.

I don't think about how devastated Danny will be when he realizes I've disappeared or how scared and worried my family must be.

On this new road, there is no room for compassion. There is no room for love or the softness and vulnerability it brings. There is only where I must go and the steps I will take to get there.

Deep down, I know this won't end well. I know I'm dooming myself as surely as the men I mean to destroy, but I can't stomach making another choice. I can either let my wound become my weapon or I can limp through life a broken person, bitter and jaded, haunted by the ghost of my innocence

Either way, the people I love are better off without me. I will never live, laugh, or love the same way again. I will never be what I was and I refuse to be the broken creature Todd and his friends created. I will forge myself anew.

I will pass through the fire of my hatred and emerge as something stronger. I will give myself time to cool and the steely edges of my new self time to harden, and then I will teach Todd, Jeremy, J.D., and Scott a lesson.

I will teach them that there is danger in preying on the weak.

You never know when a lamb will become a lion or a kitten will grow ten-inch claws.

And you never know when the person you've broken will reach down, pick up a sliver of their shattered soul, and use it to open your throat.

CHAPTER TWO

Sam

One Year Later

*"We are our own devils;
we drive ourselves out of our Edens."*
-Goethe

Someone's following me. I'm sure of it.

I pause at a vendor's stall in the Liberia Centro to survey her collection of mango wood candle-holders and cast a glance over my shoulder, discreetly searching the press of humanity filling the open air market. There is a fairly even mix of locals and tourists at the market tonight, but all of them seem too swept up in their own dramas to pay any attention to mine.

There are couples arguing or stealing kisses under the multi-colored lights strung between stalls. There are groups of girls holding up dresses and jewelry, giggling over shared jokes, and herds of young men drenched in cologne roaming the periphery, clearly more interested in the girls than the shopping. There are loud, eager vendors shouting out to passersby, old women hunched wearily on stools at the back of their crowded stalls, and younger merchants with pinched expressions, jealously observing the antics of those lucky enough to be off work and out on the town.

There are even a few women like me—twenty-somethings in khaki shorts, tank tops, and hiking boots, toting backpacks through the market, on the hunt for last minute, eco-friendly souvenirs.

I could be one of them, except that I'm not here on vacation and my backpack holds one of the world's smallest, most lightweight sniper rifles broken down into its various parts for easy transport.

But I know how to put it back together again.

I've learned a lot about the care and shooting of firearms in the past nine months. Once I'm alone in my room, I'll be able to make something deadly with the pieces I purchased from the scary man in the tattered straw cowboy hat. I'm not worried about that.

I'm more worried that my gun smuggler isn't the sensible businessman my connection in Miami assured me he was. I knew when I left my hotel with two thousand dollars in cash rolled up in an old sock that there was a chance I'd be robbed. Or robbed and shot and left in a Costa Rican alley to bleed out. I've taken self-defense and mixed martial arts and put on thirty-five pounds of pure muscle since last summer, but there's only so much a person can do when she's bringing fists to a gunfight.

Still, Carlos let me walk away, down the alley and back into the crowded Friday night market. If he'd planned to take my money and keep his gun, I don't know why he would have allowed me to surround myself with people.

I shift to my left, looking for signs of the gun and drug smuggler, but there's no one tall enough or broad enough.

The crowd is filled with soft, non-threatening looking people. Even the groups of boys with their aggressive cologne don't seem dangerous. They're hopeful teenagers looking for a hookup with a pretty girl, not predators.

But I'm sure with my newly blond hair, sun-pink cheeks, and girl-next-door face, I don't look like a predator either, and I could have any one of these people unconscious at my feet in ten seconds.

It's best to be careful and to take nothing and no one at face value.

I circle the market another time, keeping a careful eye out for any familiar faces, but I still can't locate the source of the prickling between my shoulder blades. Finally, I order a small paper bag of cheesy *bizcochos* from a vendor and wind my way out of the market onto the brightly lit streets of the town center, taking the long way back to my hotel.

Liberia, Costa Rica, is a college town, far safer and more tourist-friendly than the bustling city of San Jose to the south. But the drug cartels are still active here.

The men in my gun club in Miami say the Mexicans smuggle drugs from ports near here to the U.S. inside frozen sharks. Meanwhile, the Columbians hide their cocaine in shacks inside Costa Rica's famous national parks and grow marijuana in the valleys where eco-tours fear to tread. There is danger simmering beneath the country's natural beauty and criminals lurking in the shadows of this colonial town with its bright white buildings and tidy city parks.

I toss my grease-stained paper bag into a trash can at the edge of one such park, pausing to watch a couple arguing in a gazebo across the lawn. They're a good distance from the road, but their raised voices carry on the wind.

My Spanish is better than average, and these days I have no moral issue with eavesdropping or much of anything else. I stay long enough to realize the man and woman are fighting about where to have their wedding reception—at his parents' house, to save money, or at the bar where they met—and turn to leave. Arguing before the wedding doesn't bode well for their Happily Ever After, but the woman doesn't seem to be in danger. It's a nice change of pace.

Back in Miami, almost every time I stopped to take the pulse of a situation like that one, I ended up placing an anonymous call to the police. I always called, even if I wasn't the only witness, because I knew no one else would.

Most people are happy to avert their eyes and keep walking, as accustomed to ignoring violence as they are to expecting it.

The thought reminds me of my stepbrother, but Alec's face flits through my mind and disappears into the darkness without triggering an emotional response. I've prodded all those hurtful places in my memory so many times in the past year that my pain receptors have become calloused and numb. I don't experience any emotion the way I used to—positive or negative—but I was still glad to learn Alec wouldn't be joining the rest of his fraternity brothers on their graduation trip to Costa Rica. It helped confirm my decision that his name doesn't belong on my list.

He may have closed his eyes and pretended not to hear me scream, but he didn't actively participate. He's a coward, but I knew that the night I walked into the fraternity house beside him.

Alec's always been a coward and a liar, never one to admit his faults or acknowledge his weaknesses when he could pass the blame and squirm free of responsibility. I should have known better than to expect him to do the right thing. My own naiveté is as much to blame as Alec's cowardice and my vengeance is only for those who dirtied their hands.

I slip my backpack off my shoulder and clutch it to my chest, relishing the feeling of all the hard pieces nestled inside.

I have the gun and a few hundred rounds of ammunition. Now all I need is a little time to practice with my new weapon in an abandoned patch of jungle outside of town, and I'll be ready. By the time the Sigma Beta Epsilon brothers touch down next week, I'll be checked into the neighboring resort, have scoped out the perfect spot to lie in wait, and be ready to pick them off, one by one.

I know at least Todd and J.D. love to play golf.

As I climb the cracked marble steps to the hotel, I imagine how satisfying it will be to shoot them both through the chest as they're arguing over their score. I'm distracted by bloodlust—the only desire I've allowed myself to embrace in the past year—and not as focused as I should be.

I don't realize that the prickling feeling between my shoulder blades is back until I'm reaching for the door leading into the hotel lobby.

As soon as I sense eyes on me, I turn, searching the street in both directions.

To my right, there is a homeless man dragging a battered red wagon between a pair of garbage cans. To my left, a couple walks down the sidewalk hand in hand, a woman with a red shawl tied over her hair leans against the bus stop sign, and a flash of movement at the end of the block blurs the air as someone darts out of sight. I'm left with the vague impression that the person was tall and male, but that's it. I didn't look in time to see his face or clothing or anything that will give me a clue to his identity.

For a second, I'm tempted to run after him—if I've acquired a tail, I need to know who it is, what he wants, and how to make him go away and leave me alone—but my gun is still in pieces and the streets get darker and more dangerous in that direction.

I can't afford to get into trouble while I'm in Liberia. My only chance of getting in and out of Costa Rica without being charged with multiple counts of murder is to be sure no one learns my name or remembers my face.

I'll just have to wait, keep my eyes open, and be ready to quietly confront my stalker if he shows up again.

Cursing beneath my breath, I continue into the lobby, where an ancient air conditioner groans from the window near the front desk. The night clerk is reading something on her phone. After a glance my way and a fleeting smile, she returns to it, paying me no further attention as I cross the lobby and start up the stairs to my room.

The reviews for the hotel were critical of the lack of staff support and assistance in planning tours or navigating the city. That's the reason I chose it. I don't want support or assistance. All I want is to be ignored.

Since leaving L.A., I've mastered the art of being invisible. After a year in Miami, only a handful of people knew my name and it wasn't the one I was given at birth. I paid for my studio apartment in cash, worked under the table for a restaurant laundry service, and kept to myself. I made connections, not friends. I dyed my hair, wore a ball cap pulled low over my face, and checked to be sure I wasn't being followed when I went outside, just in case.

None of my family or former friends knew I was there, but there are a good number of street web cams in Miami. It would be easier to end up on camera and noticed by someone using facial recognition software than one would think. I didn't think even my step-mother—the only one of my three parents with enough money to hire a high-priced private detective—would go that far to find me, but I took steps to protect myself all the same.

I've been so careful, and I'm so close.

The fact that I've suddenly become a person of interest to some shadowy stranger, days from accomplishing my goal, makes me want to scream.

For the first time in months, I'm consumed with emotion, so angry my hands shake as I open the front pocket of my pack and dig out my key. It takes three tries to get the key into the lock and once I'm finally inside my room, I can't sit down.

I toss my backpack on the bed and pace the carpet between the bed and bureau, hands clenching and unclenching at my sides. I'm shocked to find myself craving a cigarette and know if I had one, I'd step out onto the pigeon-shit covered balcony outside my room to smoke.

I took up smoking to have an excuse to mingle with the other members of my gun club. I only smoked outside the shooting range and have never had the urge to light up anywhere else. I had assumed I must be immune to the addiction, but maybe I simply haven't been under enough stress to trigger a craving.

For a moment, I consider hitting the bodega a few doors down from the hotel but dismiss the idea with a sharp shake of my head.

I need to be strong, calm, and focused. I haven't let myself look further into the future than this summer or imagine who I'll be or what I'll do once I've finished this, but even in the short term, I can't afford to let my body be weakened by chemicals or addiction.

I just need to take a deep breath, calm down, and think rationally.

I fetch a bottle of water from the mini-fridge and take a long drink, focusing on the cool flow of liquid down my throat. I relax my shoulders and jaw and let my weight settle evenly between my feet.

Once I'm steady in my body, I let my mind focus on the problem at hand.

Who knows I'm in Costa Rica? Horatio—the man

from my gun club who put me in touch with Carlos—and anyone in his organization that he might have mentioned the deal to. Horatio isn't forthcoming about his alliances, but I'm pretty sure he's involved with one of the Cuban gangs running South Miami. Anyone affiliated with him would be bad news. Ditto for Carlos and whatever organization he's affiliated with, which means there is a nearly one hundred percent chance that the man following me is dangerous and that whatever he wants isn't something I'm going to be eager to part with.

So what does he want?

More money? Does he plan to rob me or kidnap me for ransom or something even more menacing?

If Carlos had a meaningful conversation with Horatio, he should have learned that I'm a loner, not well-off, and don't have any obvious ties to people with money. That would lead me to rule out kidnapping, but criminals knowing I have no one waiting for a postcard from my trip to South America presents its own problems.

I've done what I can to play down my looks—choosing modest, loose-fitting clothing, always pulling my hair back in a tight braid or bun, and limiting my makeup routine to a tube of Chap Stick—but I'm still attractive. When I first joined the gun club, a couple of the regulars tried to start something, but I quickly made it clear that I wasn't interested in that kind of relationship. I'm not vain enough to believe one of Carlos's friends took one look at me and decided I was worth pursuing, but they might have taken a look and decided I was worth selling.

The cartels traffic in people as well as drugs and, from what I've heard, make a better living at the former.

The majority of the people sold into sex slavery are young girls living below the poverty line who have slipped through the cracks in the foster system—or in some cases been forced into the skin trade by their own parents—but I'm not quite twenty-two. Not a girl, but maybe young enough to fetch a decent price on the international slave market.

I move toward the balcony, surveying the street outside through the filmy glass doors.

There's a lock on the inside I've already bolted, but it's not strong enough to withstand a firm shoulder from someone as large as Carlos. And even if it were, all an intruder would need to do is break one of the glass panes and reach inside to open the door. I'm on the third floor, but there is a fire escape with a ladder that leads to the ground. It would be as easy to come up as it would be to go down.

I noted the flaw in the room's security when I checked in, but it didn't worry me before. Now that someone is watching me, however, it would be smart to look into a more secure situation.

Unfortunately, The Allegro Hotel is laid out around a center courtyard. All of the rooms have balconies, so asking for a room change wouldn't accomplish anything. And assuming my tail has figured out which room I'm in once, he could certainly do so again.

I'm going to have to change hotels, but not tonight. It's already ten-thirty and I don't want to be out on the streets alone later than this. The search for another temporary base will have to wait until the morning. I'll just have to prepare for a potential break-in as best I can and hope I get lucky tonight.

After brushing my teeth and changing into gym shorts, I drag my large, traveler's backpack in front of the glass doors, giving anyone trying to come in through the balcony something to stumble over in the dark. Then I unpack my smaller pack and put my new toy together. The familiar activity is soothing, giving my mind something to focus on aside from the unease humming through my nerve endings.

I would prefer not to fire the gun inside the hotel, but an intruder won't know that.

The gun is small for a sniper rifle, but it's still as long as my forearm. The sight of it alone might be enough to scare him off and if not, the weapon could be used to inflict blunt force trauma as long as I get to my attacker before he gets to me.

After the gun is assembled, I turn on the television and watch the end of a Costa Rican variety show involving a surreal mix of human heads superimposed on cartoon character bodies, dancing girls in bikinis, and bad man-on-the-street interviews. A little after midnight I turn off the set and prop myself up against the head-board with the gun resting lightly across my thighs.

For the better part of an hour, I stare at the doors leading onto the balcony, watching muted orange light sweep across the glass as a car passes by on the street outside, waiting for something to happen. I figure if the person following me has been watching my window, they will wait a decent amount of time after seeing my television set turn off before making a move.

Another half hour passes and the night grows quiet.

The only sounds are the faint droning of the air conditioner far below on the first floor and the breeze tinkling the wind chimes outside the closed shop across the street. The last time I look at the clock, it reads two fifteen. I expect to stay awake to welcome three o'clock, but at some point I must have nodded off.

When I wake up, it's nearly four in the morning.

The first thing I register is the time. The second is the way the hair on my arms is standing on end.

Even in sleep, my body has sensed that something is wrong. The watched feeling has returned with a vengeance, so strong I swear I can hear another heartbeat thudding not far from my bed.

CHAPTER THREE

Sam

*T*rying not to panic, I mentally check in with my immediate surroundings.

There is no one by the door to the room, so if I need to run, that way is clear. My gun is still on the mattress beside me, just a few inches from my curled legs, so that option is available, too.

Now I just need to find out what I'm up against.

Keeping my lids slitted just enough to see, I roll over to face the balcony doors. I do my best to look like I'm still asleep, keeping my arms and legs heavy, not wanting the intruder to know I'm conscious until I make my move. Once I complete my shift in position, I intend to stay completely still. I am anticipating that the person who has broken into my room will be a man, dangerous and possibly armed, but nothing more.

I have no other expectations or suspicions.

I am entirely unprepared to see *him* standing on the other side of the patio doors, watching me through the smeared glass.

It's Danny.

Here.

Close enough to touch.

Close enough to throw my arms around him and hug him breathless.

All I have to do is open the door.

My eyes fly open and my throat locks, strangling the sound of surprise rising inside of me, transforming it into a soft whimper. But Danny hears it, and his gaze shifts, settling on my shadowed face.

"Let me in, Sam," he says softly. He looks so beautiful, so familiar. Safe, but alien at the same time, like something from another world than the one I've been living in for the past year. "I think we should talk."

Talk.

After a year apart.

After I ran from him and shut him out and severed the connection between us without even a goodbye or a note telling him I'm sorry but that I couldn't love anyone when I was filled with so much hate. After a year of knowing that he's looking for me, longing for me, and ignoring it. A year of hiding from him and the memories of the girl I was when I was with him.

I was a girl. Just a stupid little girl, playing at being a woman, thinking I understood what it meant to promise someone forever.

But I understood nothing.

Forever is impossible. Forever in a vacuum, maybe, but not forever in the real world.

The real world has too many ugly variables. It chews you up and spits you out and then goes back for seconds, gnashing you between its teeth until you barely recognize your own face in the mirror, let alone the face of the person you love. The person you *loved* when you were someone else, someone with a functioning heart, who hadn't been forced to choose between two masters.

I could never have hated the men who hurt me the way I needed to hate them if I was trying to love Danny at the same time.

Love lies. Love whispers that living well and loving well are the best revenge. It convinces you to let go, step back, and leave justice in the hands of God or karma or some other imaginary thing that will never get the job done.

If there is a God, then he let four men brutalize me and continues to allow unimaginable horror to befall innocent people every day. If that God is real, I want no part of him and nothing in my personal karma earned me a gang rape or a not guilty verdict for the men who violated me.

God and karma are lies and maybe...

Maybe love is a lie, too.

If love were real, then I wouldn't be able to look at Danny without bursting into tears and running into his arms. I wouldn't be able to cross the room and stand facing him through the glass without saying a word. Not a word, after so long. If love were real, I wouldn't be able to reach out and draw the curtain between us, shutting myself in even deeper darkness and leaving Danny on the other side.

But I do it.

I draw the curtain and then I wait, breath held, ears

straining for some sign of what he's doing on the other side.

I don't know what I'll do if he forces his way in. I was prepared for someone to hurt me—I've been preparing for that for months. I'm not prepared for someone to care or to go hunting for the girl they knew hidden inside the woman I've become. That girl is dead. I wouldn't know how to be her if I tried and I'm not going to try. I can't, not until I've finished what I've started.

And maybe not even then.

Hope, faith, and a soft heart made that girl weak. I refuse to be weak again. If I have to choose between happiness and strength, I choose strength. I choose to be hard and cold and ready to fight my own battles without anyone else to protect or disappoint.

Danny wouldn't love the person I am anyway, I think, the thought sending a sharp feeling spreading through my chest. *He should go and spare both of us an exercise in pain and futility.*

Finally, after five endless minutes that seem to stretch on for an eternity, I hear the fire escape creak as Danny climbs down to the street below. I hear the soft thud of boots on concrete as he lands and the softer tread as he walks away. Only when I'm certain he's gone do I let myself crawl back onto the bed and curl up in a ball so tight my abdomen cramps and my spine starts to ache.

I press my fist to my closed mouth and fight to steady my breath, but I don't think about Danny and I don't cry.

I haven't cried in a year and I'm not going to start now.

I am going to breathe, sleep, and then get up in the morning and try to forget I ever saw the man I used to think would be my forever.

CHAPTER FOUR

Danny

"If I love you,
what business is it of yours?"
-Goethe

*I*f this had ever been about me, I might have
kept walking.

If I'd come to Costa Rica looking for Sam, instead of
the monsters who hurt her, her dismissal would have cut
me apart. The only thing worse than not knowing where
she is or how she is or if she needs me is looking into the
big blue eyes of the woman I love and seeing...nothing.

No love. No hate. No sadness or regret.

No emotion at all aside from the clear desire for me
to leave and never come back.

I had thought I was frozen on the inside, too cold to
feel much of anything anymore, but the past two days

have proven otherwise. From the moment I spotted Sam at the airport, my pulse has been unsteady.

My heart races every time I spot her newly blond head bobbing through a crowd. My throat locks up with fear every time I watch her make another dangerous decision. And last night, meeting her eyes through the glass and realizing I mean nothing to her, I felt like I was going to die.

Maybe I did die, a little.

I feel like it.

Every muscle in my body aches, my eyes are blood-shot and throbbing, and my stomach churns and spits, protesting every drink of coffee I force down my throat. But I don't go back to my hotel room on the other side of town to sleep it off. I stay on the sour-smelling couch in The Allegro Hotel lobby, watching the stairs, waiting for Sam.

There's no other way out of her room except the fire escape and I doubt she'll go that route. She won't expect me to be here.

I almost wasn't.

I don't know how long I walked before I finally stopped and turned around, only that it was near morning and I had to take a cab back to the hotel because I was so lost. But as soon as I sat my ass down on this couch, I knew it was the right choice. My hurt and pain don't matter. There will be time to mourn the death of what Sam and I had later after I make sure she doesn't spend the rest of her life in prison.

I finish my coffee and sit staring at the peeling paint on the wall behind the lobby desk. The clerk lost interest in me an hour ago and is busy shuffling papers and typing numbers into a calculator with a printer attachment, the kind that makes a chugging sound every time he hits enter. The sound is oddly meditative, and by the time I hear familiar footsteps on the stairs, I'm as close to a Zen state as I'm ever going to achieve while I'm in the same room as Sam.

Leaning back against the mildewing cushions, I watch her descend the cracked marble stairs, by far the nicest feature of this run-down hotel. In a pair of khaki shorts and a white tank top, with her hair pulled back in a braid, she shouldn't take my breath away, but she does.

She's as beautiful as ever, more beautiful in some ways. She's always been strong, but now she's ripped, with toned arms and chiseled legs that leave no doubt she's a force to be reckoned with. And the way she holds herself, with her muscled shoulders rolled back and her chin up, is the sexiest thing I've ever seen.

My girl is beautiful and strong and determined not to take any more shit from the world.

She will always be my girl.

I will always love her, even if her love for me is one of the things she's had to burn away in order to rise from the ashes of what those animals did to her.

She shifts her gaze as she descends the stairs, not looking surprised when she spots me on the couch. She hesitates on the last step for a moment before stepping down and starting my way, but she doesn't flinch or frown.

When she stops in front of me her face is smooth and expressionless and her eyes as empty as they were last night, bulbs with burned out filaments incapable of flickering to life.

"You shouldn't be here," she says. "You should go."

"I'm here for the same reason you are." I keep my voice soft and even, despite the way my heart is racing. "We'll be better off if we work together."

Sam shakes her head. "I don't need or want your help."

"You may not want it, but you need it." I stand, looking down into her tanned face, gut churning harder as I fight the urge to reach out and touch her. It feels so wrong to be so close but still held at a distance. "I've been following you since you got here. I can guess what your plan is and it's not going to work."

"It's going to work just fine," she says with calm assurance. "I know what I'm doing. I'm not the person I was before. I know how to handle myself."

"I don't doubt it, but we can find a better way. You don't have to put yourself at risk. We can get the job done and still be free to walk away."

She tilts her chin to one side as her eyebrows pinch closer together. "What do you want?"

"The same thing you want," I say, then add in a whisper, "And I want to make sure you don't get killed or sent to prison for the rest of your life doing it. I swear I'm not here to make any demands. I just want to help."

Her frown deepens as she casts a glance over her shoulder at the clerk, whose calculator is still clicking and whirring, before turning back to me. "We can't talk about this here. I was heading out of town for the day. You can come if you want."

I nod and my shoulders relax a little for the first time since she pulled the curtain last night. "All right."

"But I'm not making any promises," she warns,

hitching her backpack higher on her shoulder. "And after we've talked, if I ask you to leave again, I need you to listen and do as I ask."

I hesitate, but finally nod again.

I'm not leaving until I know she's safe, no matter what she says, but there's no sense in having that fight right now. I learned to choose my battles when we were a couple and I sense that's an even more important skill now that we're...whatever we are now.

Nothing. You're nothing to her. She doesn't care if you live or die.

Ignoring the ugly voice in my head, I follow Sam outside into the bright morning light, where the air is already beginning to steam and the sidewalk to sizzle. Sam may not be capable of caring about me anymore, but that's not her fault. It's their fault, and maybe once they're gone, things will be different.

Or not. It really doesn't matter.

All that matters is making sure justice is served.

CHAPTER FIVE

Sam

"Know thyself?
If I knew myself, I'd run away."
-Goethe

e don't speak much on the drive out to the abandoned airstrip.

Danny stares out the window as city buildings give way to scrubby grassland on the way to the lush jungle not far from town. I concentrate on following the directions I wrote down last night and ignoring the Danny smell that fills the car, making every breath an exercise in forgetting.

Forgetting how that smell was once the best, the safest, the sexiest smell.

Forgetting what it felt like to wake up and have his spice and sea-salt scent be the first thing to fill my nose. Forgetting how I loved to burrow closer to his bare skin, press my cheek to his lightly furred chest, and relish the first few sleepy moments of the day with the man I loved.

For the first time in months, I feel the ghost of the old me shift beneath my skin, whisper through my blood.

By the time we reach the turn off to where I've planned to start my target practice, my body feels like a limb that's been asleep too long, fighting its way back to life. The humming of long-dormant sensations prickling across my skin is as unwanted as it is painful and makes me resent Danny's presence more than I did when we got in the car an hour ago.

I don't want to wake up. I don't want to come back to life.

I need to stay dead, cold, numb. I need to stay focused and having Danny around is going to make that impossible.

It doesn't matter if he approves of my plan or how much he wants to help. I need him to go. I should never have invited him to come with me today. I should have shown him the door and said whatever it took to make him leave me alone.

At the end of the dusty road leading to the old airstrip, I pull in behind a few low trees near the chain link fence and shove the car into park with a rough jerk of my arm. My jaw is clenched so tight my teeth are grinding together and I suddenly want to punch something, the way I did in the early days, right after the trial ended.

Back then, I was so full of anger I would spend hours at my punching bag, beating the shit out of the foam filled leather until I was covered with sweat and trembling with exhaustion. Some nights I wouldn't even make it to my pallet in the corner. I'd fall asleep on the floor in a puddle of my own sweat and wake up in the morning stiff, sticky, and so sore I could barely breathe.

But that was okay. There was no one there to judge or expect anything of me. It was just me, my pain, my mission, and whatever it took to keep going.

I learned to be grateful for that, to be content with the simple, spare existence left behind after everything but hate was cut away.

And now Danny is here, looking beautiful and sad, smelling the way he smells, shitting all over my focus with his gentle voice and his determined words and the way he looks at me like all he wants in the world is to hold me.

"Are you going to talk?" I snap as I reach between the seats and grab my backpack off of the floor. "I thought that was the reason you were here."

"I'm not in any big hurry," he says smoothly, unruffled by my flash of temper. "I'd like to see you shoot first. That's why we're here, right? So you can try out the gun you bought last night."

I stiffen. "If Carlos had seen you, you could have gotten us both killed. I was told to come alone and he isn't the kind of man who tolerates people disobeying orders."

"Obviously, but he didn't see me. Neither did you and I'd been following you for the better part of two days," he says. "I'm better at sneaking around than you are. Which is one of the reasons you need me."

"I don't need to be good at sneaking around. I just

need to be in the right place at the right time and have enough ammunition." I lift my chin and meet his gaze, trying not to think about how familiar his green eyes are. As familiar as my old face in the mirror, back before Todd and his friends put my metamorphosis into motion. "You might as well save your breath. I'm not going to change my mind."

Danny shrugs, one of those shrugs that could mean anything or nothing, and reaches for the door handle. "Let's go shoot something. Maybe you'll feel like listening after."

Barely suppressing a growl of frustration, I swing out of the car and slam the door behind me, leading the way down the trail twisting into the jungle without looking back to see if Danny is following. I know he is, just as I know it will be hell to get rid of him if he doesn't want to go. He's the only person I've ever met more stubborn than I am.

Or more stubborn than I used to be, anyway.

He might be surprised how far I'll go to get my point across now. I don't want to have to frighten him away, but if he leaves me no choice...

I take a deep breath and quicken my pace, not wanting to go there just yet.

According to my research, there's a shallow canyon at the end of the trail, tucked behind the old airstrip. In the forties, before the Costa Rican military was disbanded, the army used to test weapons out there.

Local gossip holds that the ground is poisoned with old biological warfare agents. The canyon is supposedly still beautiful, but the locals avoid it, and since it's on the flight path of commercial planes, the drug lords do the same.

There are no monkeys hanging from the trees pressing in on the trail, but as we get closer to the canyon, the call of toucans and the other tropical birds makes it feel like we're a thousand miles from civilization. Just around a turn, a scarlet flash flutters across the trail as a parrot lands on a low limb and fans its wings wide, stretching in the morning sun.

Danny pauses behind me, grunting softly as the bird squawks down at us from above.

Even I—as focused on the destination, not the journey, as I am—can't keep from stopping to admire the creature for a moment. I've never seen anything like it outside of a zoo or a pet store. It's so beautiful, so over the top gorgeous with its brilliant feathers that it's almost magical.

"Remember when we used to talk about surfing our way through South America?" Danny says from over my shoulder. "I brought my board. If you want to go out later, we could swap out. I hear there's a good break not far from town."

I glance at him, too stunned by the suggestion to form a response.

"Just because you're here to kill people doesn't mean you can't have a good time, too," he says, mouth curving in a lopsided smile.

I shake my head. "This isn't a game."

"I know it's not," he says, smile fading. "It's not a game, and if you get caught with that gun, you could spend eight years in jail."

My lips part, but he pushes on before I can get a word in.

"You don't even have to shoot anyone with it. Just having it in your possession would be enough." He steps closer, sending his Danny smell swirling around me all over again. "They don't fuck around with gun laws here. Even citizens have to jump through hoops to own a gun and get put in jail if they're caught with an illegal weapon."

"I'm not going to get caught."

"The Seasons has its own security team," he says. "Did you know that? And from what I've seen so far, they're better organized than the local police. If you shoot four men on their property, the chances of you getting off the property before they catch you are slim to none."

"I don't care," I say, angry that he knows something I don't when all I've done for the past year is prepare for this. "As long as I take care of them first."

"So you want to end up in jail?" His eyes narrow. "How does that even the scales? If you end up going to prison for the rest of your life for murder?"

"I told you, as long as they're dead, I don't care."

"Well you should," Danny says, heat in his tone for the first time since he showed up at the worst possible moment. "Because you deserve to have a life after this. A real life. Not dying isn't the same as living, Sam. You know that. You have to know it."

I squeeze my eyes shut, hating the sound of my name on his lips and that he has pushed me to the edge of losing control with a few stupid questions. I'm better than this, harder than this, and I have to prove it to him or he'll never leave me in peace.

With a deep breath, I open my eyes, staring up at him, willing him to believe the truth I'm about to tell. "I will never have the kind of life you're talking about again. It's too late for that."

"Why?" he asks in a strained voice. "Why do you have to go down with them? Why can't you let me help you find a way to do this that won't end in disaster?"

"I told you I wasn't strong enough to get through the trial." I know the words will cut him deep, but I force myself not to care. "But you told me to go back to L.A. and deal with the mess I'd made. So I did." I hold out my arms. "And this is what is left."

His eyebrows draw sharply together and regret flashes behind his eyes. "I wondered if you blamed me. You have every right to though, in my defense, I had no idea..."

He swallows hard. "I didn't know what they'd done and I never dreamed they'd get away with it." His eyes begin to shine. "I'm sorry, Sam, for that and everything else."

I cross my arms tight, fighting the wave of regret that swells behind my ribs. "It doesn't matter now. Like I said, it's too late. Apologies aren't going to change things and I don't want you here, Danny. I refuse to drag anyone else into this. If I'm on my own, then no one else gets hurt."

"You can't be serious." He steps closer, his breath rushing out in something too painful-sounding to be a laugh. "All I've done is hurt. Hurt and hurt and go half out of my mind wondering where you are and if you're okay. And then I saw you at the airport and I thought..."

He shakes his head, looking so lost I can't help but feel bad for him. "I thought it was a sign. That we were going to climb out of this hell together."

I cringe at the thought of "together," of how close and terrifying that sounds.

"Not like that," he says, apparently still able to read my mind. "Yes, I still love you. I'm never going to stop loving you, but if you don't want me anymore, I'm not going to push." His voice breaks on the final word, but when he continues it's steady. "I'll leave you alone, but I have to make sure you're safe first. I have to, Sam. I can't live with anything else."

He reaches up, brushing a wisp of hair that's escaped my braid away from my face, his touch so gentle it threatens to shatter me all over again. "Please. Talk to me. Really talk to me. Let me in enough to help keep you safe."

"I don't believe in safe," I whisper, resisting the urge to lean into his big, warm hand. "Safety is an illusion. No one can keep anyone else safe, no matter how hard they try."

Danny nods. "You're right, but I can keep you safer. I know I can, if you'll give me the chance. At the very least I can be your alibi."

I hesitate, my resolve wavering.

If I make it back to my hotel after the shooting without getting caught, an alibi would be a good thing to have, and Danny wouldn't have to be in any danger. He could stay in the room, and if anyone asks, he says I was there with him. Nothing dangerous about that.

Except having Danny in your room, sleeping next to you, breathing the same air, reminding you what it's like not to be alone.

"Don't answer now," he says, cutting me off before I can tell him no again. "Let's get target practice taken care of, make sure the gun's not going to explode in your face the first time you try to fire it, and go from there. And while we shoot I can fill you in on some of the things I've been thinking."

"It isn't going to explode," I say. "And you're not allowed to shoot it. My prints are the only prints that are ever going to be on this gun."

His lips curve again. "Anyone ever tell you you've got a bossy streak?"

I answer his attempt at a joke with a blank look.

I will not joke with him; I will not laugh with him. I will not let him past my defenses or give him any reason to hope for more than a brief connection before we go our separate ways.

After a moment, his smile diminishes though it doesn't completely disappear. "All right. No teasing."

"The canyon is still about a mile ahead." I hitch my pack higher on my shoulder. "We should get going. I'd like to have at least an hour to shoot before it gets really hot."

He holds out an arm, motioning toward the path. "Lead the way."

I start off again, with Danny not far behind, but I know better than to think that means I'm leading. Danny has his own agenda and he won't give up as easily as he's pretending. There was a time when he was wrapped around my finger, but I was every bit as wrapped around his. He's always been able to get to me like no one else, and I'm going to have to be very careful if I want to avoid being manipulated.

I'm going to have to remember that, no matter how familiar this feels, there is no Danny and Sam anymore.

That was the past and there is no room for the past in the here and now.

CHAPTER SIX

Danny

"By seeking and blundering,
we learn."
-Goethe

I spend an hour and a half watching Sam blast rocks of various sizes to pieces. She takes ever more difficult shots without missing, until I have to admit that as long as she's lucky enough to catch all of her targets out in the open at the same time, she has an excellent chance of taking them out.

She's an amazing markswoman, but I'm not surprised.

Sam has always been excellent at everything she does. Whether it was surfing, school, tutoring kids, or loving me, she was the best of the best.

A part of me is torn up that the girl I love is now the best at shooting sniper rifles, holding people at a distance, and staring the world's cruelest realities in the face without flinching, but I can't give in to that kind of thinking.

That's not how I'm going to win Sam's cooperation, let alone another chance at getting close to her. I have to show her that I understand what she's going through because I've walked every step through hell right beside her. We might not have been in the same time zone, but I was always with her. She was never more than a minute or two from my thoughts, even in the dark hours when I thought Caitlin might die and my baby niece along with her.

Besides, we'll both have a better chance of getting this done right if we create a new plan. My plan had holes and hers does, too, but together we should be able to come up with something that ensures punishment is dispensed while we walk away unscathed.

After Sam has burned through a box of ammunition, she joins me in the shade beneath a thickly rooted tree on the hill overlooking the canyon and pulls water and a bunch of bananas from her backpack. We share the food and drink, watching the birds return to the canyon now that the gun has gone silent. I keep my peace and give her space, waiting until I can sense her relaxing into the drowsy heat before I speak.

"There are worse things than death." I roll up my banana peel and toss it onto the dusty ground, keeping my eyes on the stunning scenery in front of us. "Both of us know that."

"There are," she agrees. "But dead men can't accuse me of a crime."

"Neither can men who have no idea you're in the

same country that they are. There are ways to make them suffer that will leave them in the dark. At least at first. I had a few thoughts about that while I was sitting here."

She takes a breath and I brace myself for another prompt to mind my own business, but instead she says, "What did you have in mind?"

"Do you think the guy who sold you the gun could get drugs, too?"

"Yes," she says, without hesitation. "He could, but why would we want them?"

"The drug laws here are even more intense than the gun laws." I cross my legs at the ankles and study my boots. "All we'd have to do is plant a kilo of cocaine on someone you'd like to see spend a decade in a Costa Rican prison and make sure the cops know where to find him."

She nods slowly. "Scott. I've been going back and forth on what to do with him. He didn't want to join in, I could tell. But he did because he'll do anything Todd tells him to do."

My mouth fills with the sour taste that always accompanies thoughts of four men taking turns violating Sam.

My Sam. My best friend who is now a stranger to me, all because of what four frat fucks started and an ignorant L.A. jury finished.

"Or we can shoot him full of so much coke he overdoses and make it look like an accident," I add in a harder voice. "If you want them dead, then they should be dead. They deserve it and it wouldn't be a waste. A man who would do something like that doesn't have anything worthwhile to bring to the world."

She glances over at me, her expression gentling. "You're a good man."

"No, I'm not." I fight the urge to take her hand and thread my fingers through hers the way I used to. "I've been daydreaming about killing them ever since I found out what happened. It's all I've been able to think about. That and if I'd ever see you again."

Her gaze drops to the dirt beneath us, where a giant beetle has found my banana peel and is crawling inside to investigate. "I wouldn't have been any good for you. But I'm sorry I didn't let you know I was okay."

Unable to resist, I lay my hand over hers, chest tightening with relief when she allows it. "You don't have to apologize. I'm the one who should apologize, for being such an asshole that last night in Taupo. I hated myself for it the next day. I haven't had a drink since."

"Me either. I don't drink anymore." She slides her hand out from under mine and stands, pacing a few steps away before turning back to face me. "So, say we get Scott sent to jail. Do the rest of them stay and finish their vacation?"

"You know they would," I say, lip curling. "They won't give a shit if one of their brothers is in trouble. They'll say he brought it on himself, call a lawyer if they're in a generous mood, and leave him to twist while they drink beer by the pool."

She nibbles the pad of her thumb. "Would a lawyer be able to get him out?"

"Maybe," I admit. "But not before he spends a year or more in jail waiting for a trial date. From what I've read, it seems like the Costa Rican courts try to be fair, but they're not real concerned with quick. There are ten U.S. citizens in the prison in San Jose awaiting trial right now. Some on drug charges, but some for smaller stuff like destruction of property or unpaid child support. All of them have been locked up more than a year."

"A year." She tilts her head back with a sigh, gazing up at the leaves whispering above our heads while she mumbles something about "going soft" that I can't quite make out.

"What?"

Her gaze returns to my face. "I can live with Scott spending a year in prison, but the rest of them don't get off that easy. J.D. and Jeremy need something worse and Todd doesn't live to hurt anyone again. He's the one who made it happen. He's the leader. Without him, the rest would have backed off."

I nod. "So we do J.D. and Jeremy—"

"*I* do J.D. and Jeremy," she corrects. "You can help with the plans and be my alibi, but that's as far as it goes. If I'm caught, I'm caught alone."

"I don't want to leave you alone." I want to pull her into my arms and hold her until the layer of frost covering her heart melts away. "Don't you think you've spent enough time alone?"

"I'm serious," she says, staring me down. "If you can't promise me you'll stay out of the serious shit and mean it, then you need to leave. I'm not going to change my mind about that."

"Fine," I agree, knowing I should be grateful I've gotten her to bend this far. "You do J.D. and Jeremy at the same time and we work out a way to make whatever happens look like an accident."

"And then we get Todd right after," she says, pacing back and forth at the edge of the shade. "Before he has time to connect the dots and realize he's the last man standing. No poetic justice for him, just something swift and final. And then we both leave the country the next day."

"Sounds good."

She turns back to me, head drifting to one side as she studies me. "Does it? Really?"

"The leaving the country part. And knowing it's finally over," I say, admiring the way the sun filtering through the leaves catches the gold in her hair. "I like the blond. I still love the brown best, but this looks good on you. Makes your eyes seem even bluer."

"Don't," Sam says, her voice soft.

"Don't what?" I ask, feigning innocence.

"You know what. That's part of the bargain too. If you stay, you stay as a partner on this project. Nothing more."

My jaw tightens. "Project is a weird word to describe framing, maiming, and killing, don't you think?"

She frowns, but I speak before she has a chance to lay down any more rules.

"I'm good with partners." I come to my feet and reach down to pick up her bag. "But I can't plot any more until I've got something more than a banana in my stomach. Let's go get some lunch. My treat."

"All right, but we get something in town, not by any of the beach resorts," she says, falling in beside me as I start back toward the rental car. "The SBE brothers aren't due to land until next week, but I've been staying away from the airport and beaches so I don't start to look familiar to people over there."

"I know," I say. "I've been following you. And watching you eat next to nothing. As far as I could tell you're running on bananas, coffee, and the occasional bag of fried cheese bread."

She lifts a shoulder. "I'm low on funds. The room at the resort next to The Seasons next week costs a fortune. I made a two thousand dollar deposit, but the rest of the balance is due at check-in. It's another four thousand and that's almost all I have left."

I curse. "That's ridiculous. Is it too late to cancel? You could come stay with me. I've got a little cabin at this hippie compound near the national park, where the company I'm working for houses their guides. It's only a five-minute drive from The Seasons."

"You're working here?" she asks, glancing up at me, obviously surprised.

I smile. "I'm on staff at Extreme Canopy Zip Line Adventure Tours for the next week and a half. They needed someone to train their staff on cliff camping and I needed an alibi. Figured it was a good match."

Sam shakes her head, but I can tell she's impressed. "You've really thought this through."

"I come from a long line of people who don't mind operating outside the law," I say, the conversation reminding me of my talk with my sister and the things she made me promise. "I wanted to go after them as soon as I found out what happened, but Caitlin warned me to wait at least a year, give them a chance to drop their guard and make sure I didn't go off half-cocked. I had a few broken fingers at the time, too, so that wasn't ideal for strangling people with my bare hands."

Sam grabs a handful of my tee shirt, holding tight as she suddenly stops in the middle of the trail.

I turn to face her, every nerve in my body prickling with awareness. She isn't even touching my skin, but this is the first time she's instigated physical contact and my gut desperately wants to believe it means something, even if my head knows better.

"I would have done the same thing for you," she says, light flickering behind her eyes, making me think maybe her heart hasn't gone dark forever after all. "I'm not that person anymore, but I remember..."

She takes a breath and lets it out slowly.

By the time the exhalation is finished, her eyes are shuttered once more and her hand has dropped back to her side. "That's why I knew I had to let you stay. And help. I would want the same if I was in your position. I can't offer much, but I can offer that."

I want to touch her so badly it's hell to keep my hands to myself.

I want to cup her face in my hands and tell her I have no doubt that she would have gone to hell and back to protect me if she could, or avenge me if she couldn't. I want to tell her that I wish it had been me. That I wish I could take everything she's suffered into myself and spare her.

I would do it in a heartbeat.

I would do anything for her.

And that's why I keep my arms at my sides and say, "Thank you," but nothing more.

Right now, Sam can't handle more. But maybe someday, when all of this is over...

She's given me no reason to hope, but I can't help it.

When you love someone the way I love her, hope refuses to die, no matter how many times it's kicked to the dirt. Hope will keep me reaching out for Sam, again and again, for as long as I have hands because there are some dreams a person can't give up on, no matter what.

CHAPTER SEVEN

Sam

"None are more hopelessly enslaved
than those who falsely believe they are free."
-Goethe

Getting in touch with Carlos again is easier than I expected.

The first time, our meeting was arranged via texts between two burner phones. I don't expect the number he gave me to work again, but only minutes after hitting send on a text asking about making another purchase—this time a sizable amount of cocaine—I get a reply.

I lean in to whisper to Danny across our table. "He says he can do a kilo for three thousand dollars."

We're at one of the many outdoor cafés near the city center. The wind is blowing and no one is seated close enough to overhear our conversation, but I'm more anxious about the drug deal than I was the gun. But then, the penalties for getting caught with that much cocaine are more severe than getting caught with an assault rifle. I'm going to be vulnerable until I unload the drugs on Scott.

It's a risk, but hopefully, as long as I'm careful, I'll be okay.

The more I think about it, the more the idea of Scott behind bars feels like the right thing. For a spineless toad like him, even a long weekend in a cage with real criminals will be enough to make him shit his pants several times over. After a year in a foreign jail, he'll be scarred for life and determined never to do anything that might land him in lock up again.

"If you cancel your reservation for next week and stay with me, we'll have enough with some left over," Danny says, pulling me from my thoughts. "Or I could pay for it. It would just be a matter of figuring out how to withdraw the cash. I've been living with Caitlin and Gabe the past year so I could help out with the baby. I've saved a lot of money not paying rent."

"How is the baby?" I ask, the question out before I think better of it.

It's not a good idea to let things between Danny and I get personal, but I can't help but wonder about the newest member of his family. I remember how excited he was, how he kept calling his sister from New Zealand to see if the baby had been born.

It feels like so much longer than a year since we landed in New Zealand, in that place where, for a few blissfully ignorant days, I thought Danny and I were going to have a chance at a future together. Where we'd been happy, despite the lies and arguments. Where we'd made love all night and then spent a perfect day on the river, feeling like all the best things in life were ours for the taking.

It hurts to remember, but I can't seem to help it, not with Danny sitting in front of me, with the sun in his hair and that familiar grin on his lips.

"Juliet is the best," he says, his love for his niece making his face light up. "Beautiful, bossy, and super smart. And she's got this laugh like a velociraptor screech from those old Jurassic Park movies. It's the wildest thing. I've got a video on my phone if you want to hear it."

I shake my head, forcing my gaze back to what's left of my plate of fish tacos. "No, that's okay."

I can't watch a video of Danny's niece and giggle with him over her silly laugh. I can't even make eye contact with him right now.

He's the kind of man who turns heads when we walk down the street—with his long blond hair pulled back in a low ponytail, handsome face, and sculpted body that manages to be elegant and intimidating at the same time.

But when he smiles like that, with all the love in his big heart on display, he's stunning. Heartbreaking.

Almost irresistible.

It's not a good idea for me to stay with him at his cabin—he messes with my focus, and at a time like this, focus could mean the difference between freedom and life behind bars—but I refuse to let him empty his savings for me. I refuse to take anything from him. I've already stolen too much.

"I'll cancel my reservation for next week and use that money to pay for the drugs," I say, determined to get us back on track. "It sounds like Carlos can meet up tomorrow, but what do I do with the coke once I have it? I can't keep it at my hotel with the maids coming in and out during the day."

Danny pops the last bite of his sixth taco into his mouth and chews thoughtfully. Clearly planning illegal activities doesn't interfere with his appetite.

"The commune is pretty chill," he says. "Just a bunch of people determined to keep their lives simple and play for a living as much as possible. My cabin is at the edge of the woods and there's no maid service. I don't see why the stuff wouldn't be safe there, but we could bury it in the jungle until we're ready to move it if you want to. Just to be safe."

I nod, pulse speeding as I pick up the phone and start thumbing a text to Carlos. "Then I'll tell him I'm good to meet tomorrow. We can head back to your place right after to hide it."

Back to Danny's place.

Soon, I'll be sleeping in the same room with another person for the first time in a year. And not just any person, but Danny, the only man I've ever made love to.

Last summer, he proved that Todd and the rest of them hadn't killed the part of me that craved physical intimacy, but that was before the trial. I haven't had so much as a hug from another human being since I left L.A., but I haven't missed physical contact. I've been cut off from my own body except in those moments when a workout or a punching session brought every cell violently to life. But that life was hard and focused, cold for all the heat pumping through my veins.

I had assumed that's who I am now, and that the trial had succeeded in alienating me from my own sensuality in a way even the rape hadn't.

Sitting in that courtroom and telling my story to a roomful of strangers, while the four men who violated me looked on with horrified expressions and insisted they were innocent, had been like living through it all again. But this time, instead of the horror being my own private weight to bear, I'd been exposed to the entire world. I'd been forced to share the ugly truth and then been branded a liar, unworthy of compassion or justice.

The experience proved to me that people, on the whole, are stupid, ridiculous, and cruel.

But Danny is none of those things.

Instead of being livid that I abandoned everything we had built without a word, he apologized for that last night in New Zealand. Instead of being too hurt to want anything to do with me, he flew to Costa Rica to punish the men who took our happiness away. After a year with no word, I am still alive in his heart, more alive than I am in my own flesh and blood.

I've been cold as stone and just as numb, but maybe, if I were to touch him, to let him in, just a little, I could come back to life.

Back to him...

The phone buzzes next to my elbow and I flinch, so startled my arm jerks forward, spilling my glass of water all over the white tablecloth.

Heart pounding, I right the glass and toss my napkin

over the mess, fighting to bring my breath under control as I rescue the phone from the path of destruction.

"You okay?" Danny asks, brow furrowing with concern.

"I'm fine," I say, teeth digging into my bottom lip as I glance down at the latest message from my drug and arms dealer. "Just thinking too hard."

"Thinking about what?"

"Nothing, stupid things." I turn off the phone and slide it into the front pocket of my backpack. "We're going to meet at four thirty tomorrow afternoon. Same place."

"If you don't want to do it, I could go in your place," Danny says. "I'd rather if you'll let me. I saw that guy. I don't like the thought of you being alone with him again."

"I'll be fine. If he was going to hurt me, he would have tried the first time," I say, picking pieces of ice from the tablecloth and plunking them back into my glass. "I think he'll want to keep me around, just to see how much more money he can get from me if nothing else. And worst case scenario, I've been training for months. I know how to defend myself."

"I can tell," he says, his gaze drifting down to my shoulders and bare arms. "I wouldn't want to mess with you."

His words say one thing, but his eyes and the husky tone of his voice say another. They say he still wants me as much as he ever did. That he'd like to know what it feels like to have my stronger, more powerful legs wrapped around him and my muscled body pressed against his, skin to skin.

I should warn him to cut it out and honor our deal to keep the personal stuff out of this.

But instead I find myself leaning closer and saying—

"No, you wouldn't. Because I would kick your ass."

His eyes flash. "Oh yeah? You think you could take me, Collins?"

"I know I could," I say. "The bigger they are, the harder they fall."

His tongue slips out, curling over his bottom lip and drawing it back between his teeth. It's his fighting-not-to-kiss me face, the one made familiar from hundreds of car rides back from the beach when we were kids, when we were sprawled in the back seat and my dad was sneaking peeks at us in the rearview mirror, making sure no teenagers were making out on his watch.

The heat in Danny's eyes makes me think about warm lips, eager tongues, and the taste of him sweet in my mouth, and for the first time in so long, I want to touch someone.

To touch *him*.

I can already imagine how perfect it would feel to have his arms around me, pulling me into his lap, kissing me senseless in front of the people bustling by on the sidewalk, talking and laughing and going about their lives as if there is nothing in the world to be afraid of. Not on a day like today, with the sun shining and a faint ocean breeze blowing in from the sea miles away and the music of street musicians filling the air with a light and happy beat.

But there are so many things to be afraid of, and if I let my shields slip, I will start to remember them all, and not the way I do now, faintly from beneath my calluses. I will be raw and vulnerable again and I can't go there. Not now. Maybe never, and Danny doesn't deserve to have hope dangled in front of him and then wrenched away.

For now, I have to stay free of any promises but the ones I've made to the men I will destroy.

So I push my chair back, moving away from Danny, no matter how much a part of me wants to do the opposite. "I'll call you tomorrow for directions to the cabin and see you after the deal is done."

"Sam, wait—"

"Thanks for lunch," I say, forcing a smile as I retreat to my hotel room to rebuild my defenses.

The next day I see Danny only for the half hour it takes to march the kilo of cocaine I've bought from Carlos back into the jungle and bury it, and for the next three days, I insist on doing as much of our communication as I can over the phone. When we have to meet in person, we meet at small cafés throughout the city, finalizing our plans in public. The only time we spend alone is during the eight miserable hours we spend in the hot sun digging a pit deep enough for a man to stand upright and not be able to peer over the edge.

At no time do I allow our conversation to get overly personal or that flirtatious lilt to enter my tone again. I am determined to protect Danny from me, even though that's clearly not what he wants.

The morning I check out of my hotel, on my way to drop my things at the cabin before Danny and I head to the airport to put our first plan into motion, I'm too nervous about the cocaine in my bag to worry about what it will be like to sleep in the same room with him again.

He promised to take the bed and give me the fold out couch. We should be safe on our separate islands, sharing the same ocean, but never getting close enough to touch. I will stay strong and learn to ignore his smell, his smile, and the way being close to him feels like treading water inches from a life raft.

I will not let him haul me in to safety.

I will stay in the water with sharks until the sea runs red with their blood, and only then will I let myself imagine what it might be like to no longer be alone.

CHAPTER EIGHT

Sam

*"Life belongs to the living,
and he who lives must
be prepared for changes."*
-Goethe

*W*hispering at café tables with Danny, the thought of coming within arm's reach of Scott Phillips and the brothers he flew in with was nerve-wracking, but not terrifying.

Most people only see what they expect to see and none of the men will be expecting me at a Costa Rican airport. Besides, my hair is a different color and I'm wearing a wide-brimmed straw hat, sunglasses to conceal my face, and a peach dress, unlike anything I've ever owned. I won't be recognizable at first glance and before Scott has the chance to do more than glance, I'll be gone.

I thought I was ready.

As ready as I would ever be to walk into an airport with a bag filled with cocaine.

But now that Scott Phillips is standing across the airy, open baggage claim at the Liberia Airport, surrounded by Sigma Beta Epsilon brothers, I'm breaking out in a sweat beneath my filmy dress. My stomach is tied in knots and my hands would be shaking if they weren't clenched tight around the coffee I've been nursing for thirty minutes.

Danny's nosing around the brothers' social media pages revealed that Todd, J.D., and Jeremy are on the next flight from L.A., landing in two hours. I don't have to worry about being noticed by my other targets, but there are fifteen brothers milling around the baggage claim and Scott is at the center of the swarm. His ever-present, pretentious, "I'm the next great American author" briefcase is right beside him, the way I expected it would be, but unless he separates from the crowd, I won't be able to get close enough to swap out our bags without attracting attention.

Seconds are ticking by and if I don't get a break soon, I won't be able to plant the drugs on Scott at the airport with its abundant supply of police ready to respond to a call from a red security phone.

Or worse, I might still be perched on this stool at the espresso bar counter with a kilo of coke in my bag the next time the burly, sharp-eyed man with the drug dog makes his rounds through baggage claim.

I spent half the day yesterday observing the man's patterns and he doesn't pass through this area more than once an hour. But it's been nearly forty minutes since I watched him lead the dog up the escalator toward the security screening line. I'm running out of time and this plan, which seemed so simple and elegant a few days ago, is beginning to look poorly thought out and far too dependent on dumb luck.

Danny and I should give up and get out of here before it's too late, but I'm possessed by the horrible certainty that if I fail now, I will continue to fail. And I can't fail. I can't, or all the hard work and sacrifice of the past year will have been for nothing.

"I should have stuck with the gun," I whisper behind my coffee cup.

"We still have time," Danny whispers back. "He'll get his suitcase and move to the back of the group. That's when you go."

I swallow, forcing the acid rising in my throat back down the way it came. "You should head back to the car. If I'm caught, I don't want you around."

"You're not going to get caught," Danny says firmly, his confidence clearly not as shaken as mine. "Look, he's got his bag. Get ready. I'll bet you dinner tonight he'll start checking his phone in two seconds. You'll be able to swing by and make the exchange without him looking up from Instagram."

I nod, heart racing as I set my coffee down and get ready to slide off my stool.

As Scott drags his black roller suitcase off the carousel, he turns to one of his friends and laughs his donkey laugh, the one that showcases his wide, blunt teeth. I thought I had control of my anger, but seeing one of the men who attacked me and lied about it going about his life like he has every right to health and happiness makes me want to kill him with my bare hands.

Heat creeps up my throat to burn my cheeks and the backs of my eyes begin to pulse and throb.

The open air baggage claim is shaded and a cool breeze stirs the air, but I feel like I'm in the middle of one of those broiling Miami days, when I would emerge from my boxing class into one hundred degree weather with one hundred percent humidity feeling like a tomato in a frying pan, so overheated I was about to split my skin.

I literally see red, my vision blurring as Scott reaches the edge of his group and keeps walking, headed toward the far side of the room.

I'm so lost in my anger it takes a beat for panic to penetrate my rage.

"Where's he going?" I ask, voice shaking. "Where's he going?"

"The bathroom. I'm going after him." Danny pulls his ball cap lower over his face and grabs the briefcase by my feet.

I snatch a handful of his tee shirt and hold tight. "No. You can't. I told you, I won't let you put yourself in danger."

"I'm not going to be in danger," Danny says, speaking low and fast. "I'm going to get this done and we're going to get out of here. Go stand by the security phone. If I touch my hat on the way out of the bathroom, make the call. I'll head out the right side of the baggage claim, giving the rest of them a wide berth and meet you at the car."

I shake my head. "Danny, no, I—"

"There's no time for a fight, Sam," he says, pressing a kiss to my cheek before he whispers, "If we're going to pull this off, we have to be prepared to improvise. See you in a few minutes."

Before I can find words to stop him, he's pried my fingers from his shirt and is headed toward the back of the baggage claim with the briefcase. He's nearly half a foot taller than Scott, with much longer legs. By the time Scott reaches the curved hallway leading into the men's bathroom, Danny is just a few steps behind.

Which is a good thing, because no sooner has he disappeared than the police officer with the German shepherd appears at the top of the elevator.

Instantly, my throat closes up with panic.

I spin to face the bar, wondering if the smell of the coke is strong enough to draw the dog into the bathroom. Just in case, I fumble my phone from the burlap purse slung across my body and stab out a quick text to Danny—

Dog back. In baggage claim. Don't come out with bag.

—and hit send, only to be rewarded with a hum from the stool beside me. I glance down to see Danny's phone resting on the metal seat.

It must have fallen out of his board shorts again.

Shit.

Shit, shit, shit.

Doing my best to appear calm and in control, I slide Danny's phone into my purse along with mine, leave a few hundred *colones* by my coffee cup for the harried woman manning the counter alone, and start across the room to the emergency phone.

I keep my pace slow and even, ignoring the sweat

beading on my upper lip and the hair rising on the back of my neck. The return of the policeman and his dog are bad news for calling in a report, too. I planned to make an anonymous tip and don't want to be seen, but getting caught with the phone in my hand is far better than Danny getting caught with the drugs.

Stomach cramping and my pulse fluttering unhealthily in my ears, I lean against the concrete wall a few yards from the phone, gaze fixed on the exit to the bathroom, willing everything to be all right.

The policeman and his dog are taking their sweet time circling each of the carousels and almost all the SBE brothers have their bags. It feels like it takes hours for Scott to emerge, dragging his suitcase behind him. I push away from the wall, heart slamming against my ribs as I try to get a better look at the other bag he's carrying.

He's only a hundred feet away, maybe less, but the briefcase is in his right hand and I can't see enough of it to be sure which one it is—his old, battered case, or the new one we bought and roughed up to match it. My hands clench and unclench at my sides as Scott hurries to rejoin his friends and the policeman and his dog complete their circuit of carousel three and start toward the final carousel, their path leading them directly past the bathrooms.

If Danny comes out with the drugs right now, he's going to be caught. There's no way the dog is going to miss a kilo of cocaine gliding by right beneath its nose.

I press my lips together and hold my breath, praying for the first time in longer than I can remember. I don't know who or what I'm praying to, only that I need

Danny to be okay. I can't let him go to jail because of
me. Knowing he's locked away in a cell and suffering
because he loved me too much to let me flush my life
down the toilet alone would make the hell of the past
year seem like a walk in the park.

In that moment, as I wait for Danny to emerge and
the dog lifts its nose, its muscled body tensing as it
scents the breeze drifting through the airy archways
leading to the road, I realize how much I still love him.

My mind clears and the barbed wire coiled around
my heart falls away and I'm flooded with love.

And regret.

How could I have let him do this? I should have
wrapped my arms around him and refused to let go. I
should have tackled him and wrenched the bag out of
his hands.

Right then, I swear I will do whatever it takes to
keep him safe, if only he steps out of the bathroom
holding Scott's bag instead of his own.

A moment later, Danny's familiar form appears in the
open doorway and time slows. His head is tipped down,
his face concealed by the brim of his ball cap, so I have
no idea what he's feeling. The bag in his hand doesn't
look like the bag we bought at the office supply store,
but it's hard to tell at this distance. It could be the case
with the coke in it, and if it is, I need to get it in my
hand before the dog discovers the source of the smell
making its large ears stand straight up and the hair on its
back bristle.

I propel myself away from the wall, walking as fast as
I dare toward Danny, planning to wrench the briefcase
from his hand and accuse him of stealing it if that's the

only way to make sure I take the fallout for our failed plan. But before I'm ten feet from the emergency phone, the dog lets out a deep, terrifying bark and leaps forward.

It lunges for Danny, towing its bulky handler behind it.

I freeze, eyes going wide and terror overloading my nervous system. For a moment, I'm afraid I might do something spectacularly ineffective and girly like faint, but then the dog keeps going. It charges past Danny—who is tugging the brim of his hat as he ambles toward the opposite side of the baggage claim, looking every bit the laid back surfer without a care in the world—and aims its powerful body at Scott.

I watch as the dog rips the briefcase from Scott's hand, shaking it in its powerful jaws until the top flap flies open and a dark green, plastic wrapped kilo of cocaine comes tumbling out.

Thank.

God.

Or whoever is listening to dark prayers like mine.

Biting back a cry of relief, I turn to the right, moving away from the drama unfolding by carousel four. Out of the corner of my eye, I see the cop draw his gun and order Scott to the floor, first in Spanish, then in louder, more authoritative English.

"There's been a mistake," Scott says, paling as he lifts his hands into the air. "I didn't do anything wrong. I don't know what that is. It's not mine!"

The second part of his protest is true enough, but Scott has done his share of wrong things.

Of wicked, heartbreaking, life-shattering things.

As he's forced to the ground and his arms pulled roughly behind his back, I don't feel the slightest flash of conscience. This is what the spineless worm deserves. This is better than he deserves. He's getting off easy though he obviously doesn't know it.

By the time the officer has the cuffs locked around his wrists, Scott is crying out for his friends to help him, begging someone to come explain that there's been a horrible mistake. But the rest of the Sigma Beta Epsilon frat keep their distance, watching their brother get arrested with expressions ranging from shock to amusement to the boredom peculiar to the very rich and poorly brought up.

Scott is at the bottom of the Greek social structure, a legacy whose father donated too much money to Sterling University's SBE house for his son to be denied membership. Scott is tolerated by his brothers, allowed to fawn and flatter and to do the jobs the others don't have time for. He's the one who organized the cleaning for the house and made sure the kegs were picked up in time for the parties. He's the one who kept records on the pledges and filled out paperwork for the Greek council. He's the type of guy who can't say no, whether it's signing on for another thankless job or stepping in to take his turn raping a girl pinned to a pool table because his frat president told him to.

He's pathetic, and if circumstances were different, I might feel sorry for him. He will never be man enough to be anything other than bottom dog, a cowering, self-hating omega begging for scraps from monsters he believes are his betters.

But I remember the way he whimpered as he shoved

inside the already wounded place between my legs, grunting like a pig as he found release to the cheers of his brothers. I remember watching him stumble away to collapse on the floor against the wall, tucking himself back into his pants with shaking hands, looking like he was the one who had just lived through something unspeakable. He'd kept his gaze on the floor and his chin tucked to his chest, refusing to look up or meet the eyes of the person he'd violated.

Because I remember, because I will never forget, no matter how much time passes or how much distance I get from that night, I turn my back on Scott and walk away.

And with every step I take toward the parking lot, I feel a little freer.

I lift a hand, holding my straw hat firmly onto my head as I step out of the baggage claim into the breezy afternoon, one less shadow following me into the sun.

CHAPTER NINE

Danny

*"If you've never eaten while crying,
you don't know what life tastes like."*
-Goethe

It took an insane amount of self-control to keep from busting into the stall where Scott was taking a dump and beating him bloody.

I wanted to see his pasty face slack with fear.

Then I wanted to listen to him scream as I shoved the kilo of cocaine up his ass.

I knew when I boarded the plane to Costa Rica that seeing the men who hurt Sam wasn't going to be easy, but I hadn't counted on the overwhelming instinct to destroy. It was like the need to inhale after too long underwater, painful to resist and so wrong feeling that the primitive part of my mind howled at being denied its right to deliver pain.

Scott deserves to hurt. The hurt should flow from my fists to his body, until he feels, in a visceral way, all the misery and trauma he's inflicted.

I wanted to extract my vengeance from his flesh so badly I had to bite down on the inside of my cheek to keep from climbing over the stall divider and going after him. Instead, I walked calmly into the stall next to his, set the briefcase down on the floor between his stall and mine, and took a piss. When I finished, I flushed, unlocked the door behind me, and let it bang open, hoping the sound would draw Scott's attention away from the ground as I reached down and grabbed the handle of the wrong bag.

His bag.

I was headed to the exit, but at the last minute reversed direction, walking softly to the back of the long bathroom, where I locked myself in the handicapped stall and stepped up on top of the closed toilet seat. There, I disposed of all Scott's personal effects—laptop, spiral notepad, pens, three different kinds of gum, ear buds, and a crumpled boarding pass—in the garbage and waited to see what he would do next.

If he realized he had the wrong briefcase, I was guessing he would rush out into the baggage claim area to find the man who had taken it. He wouldn't imagine that I was still in the bathroom, a fact I'd take advantage of to emerge quietly behind him and disappear in the opposite direction while he wasn't looking.

Holding my breath, I listened as the bastard finished shitting and rolled his suitcase out of the stall. He stopped to wash his hands, seemingly not in any hurry to leave the bathroom.

I thought, if my luck held, he wouldn't realize a switch had been made until I was in the parking lot and he was being arrested by the Costa Rican police.

*W*alking out of the bathroom and getting a front-row seat as the drug dog snatched the bag from Scott's hand and the cop forced him to the ground was an unexpected gift.

I can't remember the last time I felt this fucking good.

My gait, as I cross the hot pavement, is loose and easy, but inside I'm soaring. I want to lift my fists into the air and let out a shout of triumph. I want to run laps around the parking lot until I purge myself of all the excess energy pumping through my blood. Most of all, I want to snatch Sam up in my arms and swing her in circles until she laughs and begs to be put down. I can't wait to share this victory with the only person in the world who can understand how much I needed it.

When she joins me at the car, popping the trunk so I can toss the briefcase inside, I can barely keep my hands to myself.

But I know we need to get out of here. Pausing to celebrate too soon would be a mistake.

"Did you see?" she asks, her excitement clear in her voice as we get in and buckle up. "I didn't even have to call it in, so there won't be anything to make it look like it was a setup."

"I saw. It was beautiful." I glance back over my shoulder at the terminal. "I just wish we could have stayed and heard him scream some more."

"Me too." Sam's breath rushes out, but she doesn't speak again until she's paid for our one hour of parking and pulled out onto the road. "But that was way too close. I saw the dog coming and tried to text you, but your phone had fallen out of your pocket. I almost lost it. I thought you were going to jail and it was going to be all my fault."

"It wouldn't have been your fault," I say, not bothered by the close call for some reason. I know there is no great and powerful force watching out for me and mine, but right now it feels like fate or destiny or something bigger than myself is on my side. *Our* side. "It would have been my fault for wearing shorts without Velcro pockets."

Sam tosses her hat into the back seat, shaking her hair loose.

This is the first time I've seen it down. Despite the new color, she looks more like the old Sam, making it even harder to resist the urge to touch her.

"Seriously, Danny," she says, her worried gaze divided between the road and me. "We agreed that I would be the only one in the line of fire and then you went and put yourself in danger at the first opportunity. That's not okay."

"Come on, Sam, I did what I—"

"You have to promise you won't do anything like that again," she says. "I can't have you hurt or in jail. I wouldn't survive it. In fact, it's probably better if you leave right now."

"Pull over." I point to the road ahead of us.

"I can't, we need to—"

"Pull over," I insist. "Down that gravel road right

there. I need to explain something and I can't do it while you're driving."

She hesitates, but finally, with a huff of irritation, she slows and turns right. She keeps driving, rolling on for maybe half a mile before pulling over to the side of the road beneath three Guanacaste trees spreading their mushroom heads out to shade the dusty gravel. She glances in the rearview mirror and does a quick scan of the woods on one side of the road and the sugar cane field on the other before rolling down the windows and cutting the engine.

"What is it?" She's frowning and her mouth is tight, but I can see something in her eyes, something I was afraid I might never see again.

It's my soft Sam, with her big heart, who would do anything to protect the people she loves. She's wounded and limping, a shadow of the person she used to be, but she isn't gone. She's still there and I'm not giving up until I make the world safe for her again.

"I promised to keep my hands clean so you wouldn't fight me about sticking around to help," I say. "But now it's time to cut the bullshit."

Her frown deepens. "It's not bullshit. I don't want you in danger."

"It doesn't matter which of us is in danger. What's done to you is done to me." I lean in, holding her gaze, willing her to feel the misery that's been my constant companion since I learned what happened to her and then lost her. "Can't you see that? Your pain is my pain. If you're behind bars, I'll never be free. If you're hurting, I can't be happy. I'm not built that way."

Her brow smoothes and regret creeps into her

expression. "I was trying to spare you. I didn't want to drag you down with me."

"It doesn't matter what you wanted. You're a part of me. Where you go, I go." I cup her cheek in my hand, brushing my thumb over her beautiful mouth.

"But neither of us is going down anymore," I continue in a rough voice. "We're on our way back up."

"You think so?" Her eyes begin to shine. "Do you think that...once it's over, I might be okay again?"

"I won't stop until you're okay," I promise, leaning closer. "Better than okay. And nothing in the world could make me leave you, so don't ask me again."

She swallows. "I haven't cried since the trial."

"Cry if you need to. I don't mind."

"I don't want to," she says, her gaze dropping to my lips. "I want to kiss you, but..."

"But what?" I hold my breath.

"I'm afraid," she whispers. "I don't know if I'll ever be good for you again."

"As long as you're with me, I'm good," I say, my throat tight. "Or at least better."

I shake my head, not wanting to think about what a wreck I've been. "I've been so messed up, Sam. Nothing feels real without being able to share it with you. You're a part of me, and I'd rather cry every day with you than try to learn how to laugh without you."

Her eyes squeeze closed. "I hate that. I hate that I stole your happiness away. I'm so sorry."

"You didn't steal anything." I capture her chin, pressing my fingers into the bone until she looks at me. "They stole from both of us and now we're going to take everything back. Our happiness, our future, everything."

Doubt flickers in her eyes, but her hands come to rest on my chest, sending heat and hope rushing across my skin. "I can't make you any promises. I can't even think about the future until this is over."

"Then don't think," I say, my lips moving closer to hers. "Feel."

My mouth settles over hers and her lips part with a sigh so sweet and sad it threatens to break my heart.

The world stands still and then, slowly, the clock reverses.

Time rewinds, stripping away the months we've spent apart, taking us back to before the trial, before our failed escape, before Sam returned to school for that last terrible semester.

We go back to our perfect Christmas and the fierce, perfect, wild love that lived between us. To those days when forever was practically in our hands and all of our dreams were a whisper away from coming true. Her tongue seeks mine with a hunger that echoes through my bones and her taste floods through my mouth, bringing back memories of every kiss, every touch, every time I made love to this woman who owns me, body and soul. Her arms twine around my neck and her breath comes faster as, one by one, all the barriers between us come crashing down.

I circle her waist with one arm and drive my free hand into her hair, needing to be closer, to disappear into her and never be found.

I never want to stop kissing her.

I never want to be without her again, this person who is as much my family as anyone bound to me by blood.

Hell, she's more precious to me than half the people who share my DNA. Because I chose to love her, because she won my devotion with every act of heart and bravery, from the day she took a punch for me when we were kids, to the day she left me in a hotel to fly back to face her demons alone, determined to spare me the horror of being in that courtroom with her.

"I love you," she whispers against my mouth, making my heart cry out with relief so profound it's painful. "So much."

Tears fill my eyes and my arms wrap tighter around her, pulling her over the gearshift and into my lap.

"I wish I'd been there," I say as she curls into me, her face tucked into the curve of my neck. "I wish I'd been in the courtroom. I could have testified. I could have convinced them you weren't the person they were making you out to be."

"I doubt it," Sam says, pressing a kiss to my throat. "And I'm glad you weren't there. I didn't want you to see me like that. If I'd known you were listening, it would have made it so much worse."

"I know everything. I couldn't stop reading about it." I swallow against the lump rising in my throat. "I wish I'd been able to protect you. Or at least been there for you. After."

"I didn't let you be there." She pulls back, looking at me, her expression vulnerable. "But I'm glad you're here now. Can you ever forgive me?"

"I already told you, there's nothing to forgive."

"No, there is," she insists, eyes shining. "I was so numb. To everything. I knew I missed you, but I didn't realize how much. If I had, I would have known how badly you were missing me, too."

"Missing is a gentle word for it." I smooth her curls away from her face. "Lost is a better one."

"Lost," she echoes. "Yes."

"But now I've found you and everything is going to be okay," I say, cupping her cheek in my hand. "I promise."

Our eyes meet and slowly, bit by bit, I see her resistance fade. I see the moment she begins to hope and it makes me feel like someone set butterflies loose in my chest. It isn't belief, but it's a start, and it feels like the world is finally on its way to being right again.

There's only one thing that could make this moment better.

"Can I take you surfing now?"

She laughs, a real Sam laugh, one of the sounds I've missed the most in the past year.

"What?" I ask when she's still giggling a minute later. "What did I say?"

"Nothing," she says, smile still in place. "I was just thinking it would be nice to catch a few waves. Unwind a little after all the crazy back there."

"Great minds think alike." I run my hand up and down her thigh, loving the way the thin fabric makes it feel like I'm touching her bare skin. I don't have any intentions of rushing things—I'll wait as long as it takes for her to feel ready for more than a kiss—but it's so good to be able to touch her without her shying away. "I think we deserve the afternoon off to celebrate. One down, three to go."

Worry creeps back into her expression. "Do you

really think we'll be able to pull the rest of it off without getting caught?"

"I do, but I like to see you worrying about getting caught."

She arches a brow, "And why's that?"

"Because it means you're realizing you've got a lot of things to look forward to," I say, squeezing her leg, not missing the way she shivers in response. "Let's get out of here. I've got a staff meeting tonight, but we've got plenty of time to hit the break and get back before dinner."

"All right," she says, sliding back into the driver's seat. She starts the car and shifts into drive, but before she pulls out, she reaches out and threads her fingers through mine. "Thank you."

"You're welcome."

We hold hands all the way back to the cabin and that simple thing is enough to make me feel like a lucky man.

CHAPTER TEN

Sam

"Enjoy when you can,
and endure when you must."
-Goethe

We reach the beach just after two o'clock when the morning sun worshippers are packing up to head into town and the afternoon surfers are gearing up to hit the bigger waves as the tide comes in.

The beach is breathtaking—white sand more powdery than what I'm used to, gently swaying palm trees, and a grassy area where locals are grilling and little kids are running around with kites the wind threatens to snap in two. The break is about a hundred yards from the shore, and the ocean floor between the beach and the best surfing is splotchy with coral hidden beneath the waves.

To our right, the sheltered cove ends in a cliff that soars straight up from the sand. To our left, a series of dark, jagged rocks jut up from the ocean like a rotten set of teeth. They make it look like the shoreline is grinning at the surfers, daring them to glide a little closer and get chomped to bits.

Danny rents a second board from a guy with dreads hanging out in the shade near the parking lot, and we head down to the ocean to paddle out.

The warm water, bright sun, salty breeze, and the flash of Danny's strong arms paddling in my peripheral vision, combine to give me a killer case of déjà vu. For a moment, I feel like the person I used to be. Like the girl who couldn't wait to spend the weekend bumming around the beach with her boyfriend, eating too much calamari at the Fish House for dinner, and walking home with his hand in hers and the smell of sun-warmed skin and her favorite person swirling all around her, making her feel like any place she went with him would be home.

But the moment fades, the way moments like that always do.

No matter how good it feels to be with Danny or how much I'd like to go back to how we used to be, I'm still the new me, a woman who will never find peace until I finish what I've started.

All the way out to the break, I can't seem to pull my eyes away from the jagged rocks. An inexperienced surfer could get into a lot of trouble at a break like this. It would be so easy to get pulled right instead of left and end up surfing your way into a few broken bones, a concussion, or worse.

I imagine what it would be like to watch J.D. and Jeremy wipe out on that evil, grinning reef though I know that isn't the answer to the question of what to do with them. I'm not sold on Danny's idea—though I hate to waste the day we spent digging that damned pit—but a surfing accident isn't a good alternative.

We need something simple. Simple, but nearly deadly, that will make sure they never touch a woman without consent again. I don't care if Scott knows why he's being punished—he's too dumb to learn from his mistakes, anyway—but the rest of them need to know why they're suffering.

Danny and I reach the lineup and straddle our boards, bobbing up and down on the waves as we wait our turn to paddle into the break. I twist my hair back into a damp ponytail, pulling my gaze away from the rocks to find Danny watching me.

The expression on his face makes me feel hot all over and the sun beating down on the glittering water has little to do with it. The love and longing in his eyes make my chest ache with regret for what I put him through, but it also makes my skin tingle. I'm suddenly aware of the wind caressing my damp skin, the taste of salt and Danny's kiss lingering on my lips, and the fact that I fill out my swimsuit in a different way than before.

I've always been in good shape, but now my body is a monument to willpower and revenge. I've only gone up one clothing size, but I've gained almost forty pounds of pure muscle and there is very little softness left on my frame. I know some men would find my broader shoulders and tightly muscled arms and legs unattractive, but I can tell Danny appreciates the view.

He's looking at me like he'd like to stretch me out on the sand and kiss every inch of my skin and for the first time since last summer, I think I might like that.

I might like it *very* much.

I came to Costa Rica to exorcise the demons that had driven me to run away from everyone I loved. I knew I was capable of hurting the men who had hurt me, but I never thought I'd find my way back to all the things I'd lost. I was certain I was too far gone, too damaged to ever be whole again.

But maybe I'm not.

And maybe it's okay to let myself soften, just a little.

"What are you thinking?" Danny catches the edge of my board, drawing me closer.

I lift one shoulder and let it fall. "About you. About this."

I rest my hand on his thigh and squeeze, feeling the strength of him beneath his damp board shorts. "You've put on some muscle."

"Exercise helped curb the urge to punch things." He smiles ruefully. "Last summer, I tried to put my fist through a brick wall and broke my hand. I figured that had to stop if I was going to be in good enough shape to take care of business, so I started hitting the gym instead."

"How is the business?" I ask. "Did you ever open the location in Maui?"

"No, not yet. But I wasn't talking about that kind of business." His gaze drifts over my shoulder. "I wonder if anyone offers surfing lessons out here. That reef looks dangerous. A newbie could get in trouble pretty quick. Especially if they had a push in the wrong direction."

I blink. "Were you reading my mind?"

He shifts his attention back to me with a wink that makes my stomach flip. "Maybe. A little. It could work."

I shake my head. "No, it couldn't. You'd have to make contact with them. That's the same reason I'm on the fence about you taking them to the pit. Even if they don't have enough evidence to press criminal charges, their families are rich. If they can describe what you look like, they could hire someone to hunt you down."

I brace my hands on my board and shift my legs under the water as a larger wave lifts us up and sets us back down. "Besides, there are too many variables with a surfing accident, too much left up to chance."

"No variables with a big ass hole in the jungle filled with vipers," he says, in a matter of fact voice that makes me laugh, no matter how twisted this conversation is.

"What?" His eyes crinkle at the edges, making me want to kiss each tiny smile line, just to show how grateful I am that they're still there. "I'm serious. It doesn't matter if they see my face. We've already got the hole. It would be a shame to waste it. And there's a creeper who sells snakes living just down the road from the compound."

He dips a hand in the water, using his damp fingers to smooth the hair away from his face. "I say I trick J.D. and Jeremy into a free canopy tour, drop them in the pit with the snakes, and tell them they're there to pay for the terrible things they did. Then we give them an hour or two to freak out that they're going to die of snake bite before we call the paramedics."

I mull it over again, hands returning to my board as

another large wave surges by. "Are you sure there isn't a way to do it without you making direct contact?"

"I don't know. Maybe we can figure something out. If we put our heads together," he says, attention drifting to my mouth. "And our lips. I could kiss you for another hour or two tonight if that's something you'd be interested in."

I trap my tingling bottom lip between my teeth as I nod.

"And how about sleeping in the bed with me tonight?" he adds, hurrying to clarify, "Just sleep, that's all. I've just missed waking up with a mouthful of curls in the morning."

I can't help but feel sad that Danny thinks he has to be so careful with me.

This was what I was afraid of last summer, that our love would never be the same once he knew what had happened. That the men who hurt me would always be in bed with us, making him treat me like I'm made of glass.

But after a moment, I push the anxious thoughts away. We'll cross that bridge when we come to it. For now, I want to enjoy the afternoon and look forward to a night in his arms.

"Sounds good," I say, feeling a little shy as I add, "I've missed waking you up to tell you to stop snoring."

"I've missed that, too. I've been sleeping way too soundly without someone around to jab me with her bony finger and growl at me to shut up."

"I don't growl," I protest. "I ask nicely."

"You growl. But I like it," he says, grinning as he lies down on his belly and turns himself around to face the beach in advance of the set rolling in. "I like your feral side."

"I'm going to show you my feral side." I reach out to smack his ass, but he's already pulling hard, building up speed to catch the next wave.

He drifts out of reach with a laugh so infectious I can't help laughing with him. I get into position and ride the next wave in, coasting past Danny just as he falls sideways into the surf, knowing better than to jump off feet first with urchin-studded coral under the water.

After more than a year without a surfboard beneath my feet or a flight across the water, my first ride is delicious. Fast and free and light-up-my-bones perfect. I don't ever want it to end. As I start to slow, I inch toward the top of the board and lean forward, hanging on for another hundred feet.

By the time I lean back and sit down, I'm close enough to see the faces of the people on the beach, close enough to see the jeep full of polo-shirted college boys pulling into the parking lot, parking two spaces down from my own rental car.

Even before I catch a glimpse of his profile as he slams out of the driver's side of the jeep, I know the man in the blue shirt is Todd.

There's something about the way he holds himself, like he knows nothing in the world can touch him, that is different than the average frat jerk. In his mind, Todd is a god, above the law, above the rest of us, and deserving of the right to do whatever he pleases and get whatever he wants.

His is the face I see on the devils in my dreams.

His is the voice I hear in the darkness, promising to

come for me again, swearing that I'll never be sane, never be safe.

The sweet freedom from a moment before curdles inside of me, filling my mouth with the sour taste of terror as I turn my board around and paddle away from the shore. I can't let Todd see me. I can't let him know I'm here. J.D. and Jeremy are stupid enough to believe in crazy coincidences, but Todd is a predator. He'll take one look into my eyes, see the hate glowing there, and know I'm here for one reason.

And then he'll do whatever it takes to keep himself safe and I'll never finish what I've started.

"He's here," I say, breath coming in harsh gasps as I draw up beside Danny. "He's here. On the beach."

Danny's smile fades. "Who? Todd?"

I nod, as frantic as if I'd spotted a shark in the water near my board. "What are we going to do? There's no way back to the car without going by the beach. He'll see my face and he'll know. He'll know Danny, he'll—"

"It's going to be all right." Danny squeezes my hand, holding tight as a wave washes over the top of our boards. "We'll paddle around the cliff. Maybe there will be a smaller beach on the other side. If not, at least we'll be out of sight while we hang out and wait for them to leave. They won't stay long. There's no beer for sale here and frat boys on vacation are going to need a beer in their hand before five o'clock."

"Okay," I say, pulse slowing a bit in response to the calm, logical tone in his voice. "I'll follow you."

"We'll go together," he says. "I'll stay between you and the beach just in case. They're not going to see you and they're not going to hurt you, Sam. I promise. I'm never going to let anyone hurt you again."

"Let's go," I say, paddling toward the cliff, knowing now isn't the time to have an argument with my knight in shining armor.

I love Danny for wanting to stand between me and danger and have always admired his brave heart. But he doesn't understand how dangerous Todd can be. He didn't sit in the courtroom and watch the monster lie with such conviction that the jury believed his outrageous falsehoods over my simple truth. He didn't see the look on Todd's face as he watched his friends take turns with me. Todd was the only one who wasn't afraid to look me in the eye, who was capable of staring straight into my tear-streaked face and smiling.

He craved my pain. It was my suffering that got him off, not my body.

Todd is a menace, an evil thing set loose on the earth, and the biggest threat to my future. Only when Todd is dead, when I know I'll never have to see his face and never have to fear his touch, will I be able to truly move on.

CHAPTER ELEVEN

Danny

*"We are shaped and
fashioned by what we love."*
-Goethe

*S*am and I spend a tense half hour floating in the increasingly dramatic waves rolling into the shore before I paddle back around the cliff to find that the red jeep Sam saw has been replaced by a beat up blue pickup truck. By the time I paddle back to get Sam, we carry our boards in, rinse off, get her board returned and mine strapped to the top of the rental car, there is barely time to get back to the compound before my meeting with the staff.

I hate leaving Sam alone in the cabin, even for an hour, but I have to do the job I came here to do. If I don't, we'll lose our safe haven from the hotel maids.

And I still believe the overnight training session could be important for establishing an alibi.

I know Sam and I will both be careful, but when it comes to a murder charge, an airtight alibi can mean the difference between life and death.

Death.

The entire time I'm talking ropes and harnesses and demonstrating the backup security procedures for lashing a sleeping ledge to a cliff face to the other guides, I'm thinking about Todd Winslow. The lag while I wait for what I've said to be translated into Spanish, for the staff members who don't speak English, gives me plenty of time to remember the terror on Sam's face when she realized he was on the beach.

He's the ringleader, the one who set this nightmare in motion. Without him, the other three might have wanted to take turns with a girl, but they wouldn't have dared to do it.

Todd is a sociopath. Maybe even a psychopath. At twenty-one, he led the gang rape of an innocent woman and walked away from the trial without a smear on his reputation. Who knows what he'll be doing by the time he's thirty. I know he won't get better with age and that Sam will never fully recover as long as that evil shit is walking the earth.

He has to die and I'll have to be the one to kill him.

I know Sam's physically stronger than she was and insanely good with a gun, but she shook for a good ten minutes after we'd paddled out of sight of the beach today. She isn't as ready for this as she thinks she is.

But why should she be, after what they did to her?

I think about it every time I see a guy in a fucking

polo shirt with Greek letters on his ball cap. I think about a bunch of smug, entitled assholes ganging up on my girl, holding her down while they use her for a night's entertainment, not giving a shit about the life they're ruining or the good person they're tearing apart.

Fraternities should be burned to the ground. They bring out the worst in people who aren't that enlightened to begin with. Any prick who needs to spend a shitload of money to buy "brothers" is only half a man, and people who aren't whole too often fill the void inside of them with dangerous things.

During the year Sam and I spent apart, I almost picked up a bottle at least a dozen times.

On those long nights, when I lay in bed feeling so lonely and sad I wasn't sure I wanted to be alive anymore, the oblivion I knew I'd find at the bottom of a fifth of Jack sounded pretty damned good.

But then I would think about that last night with Sam in New Zealand and all the cruel things I said to her after I drank those bottles of wine and I would go for a run or a swim, instead. And while I ran or pulled hard through the water I would think about luring Sam's attackers into the middle of nowhere and torturing them to within an inch of their lives.

That is how I filled the hole inside of me and I will use that hatred now, to end Todd before he can hurt anyone else.

"Do you think so, Danny? That harnessed is the best way?"

I turn to see Paola, the trilingual Italian girl serving as my translator, looking up at me with an expectant expression. Knowing I've been caught zoning out, I grin and run a lazy hand through my hair.

"I'm sorry, P." I play up the dumb surfer bit, wanting to make sure the other tour guides remember me as a laid back guy way too chill to have killed someone. "I was already halfway up the mountain in my mind and missed the question. What was it again?"

Paola repeats the question, we chat with the other guides for a few minutes about the importance of keeping all campers in their harnesses and secured to the rock face, even when it's time to head into the tents for the night, and then we break for iced coffee and Galletas Maria cookies. I spend another thirty minutes hanging out, shooting the shit with the other guides, pretending to be psyched about our first training expedition tomorrow.

Only when most of the others have retreated to their cabins, do I grab extra cookies for Sam and head back across the compound.

The sun has set, but pale orange light still lingers in the air, illuminating the dust motes drifting by on the breeze, giving the three monkeys hanging out in the tree next to our cabin a glowing, fuzzy halo around their little heads. I pause to watch them, amazed all over again at how strange and exotic this part of the world feels to a person who has never spent time in this kind of tropical rain forest.

I've been all over Europe and spent every summer since I was a kid on Maui with Sam, but I've never been somewhere that feels so wild and primal. Costa Rica is beautiful, but it's also a place where it's easy to get in touch with fears and desires that have been lingering below the surface, ignored until they're sweated out in the jungle heat.

It is the perfect place to commit a murder.

It's also the perfect place to fall in love again.

I head up the stairs to the cabin, wondering if it's possible for me and Sam to have one without the other, if we will be able to recapture what we've lost if we fail to finish what we've started.

"I brought cookies." I swing through the front door, forcing an upbeat note into my voice, pretending I haven't been dwelling on the best way to murder a man for the past hour and a half.

But my performance plays to an empty room.

Fear that Sam has changed her mind about being a team and left to do something crazy on her own makes my stomach clench, but then I see the note on the dining table.

I went down the river trail to that hot spring they were talking about. Come join me when you're through. I have towels and bug lanterns.

Just bring yourself.

Swimsuit optional ;).

Aside from when we were kissing in the car earlier, my cock's been fairly well-behaved the past few days. I know Sam's not in a good place and as much as I want to be with her again, sex is pretty much the last thing on my mind. I'm more preoccupied with revenge and wondering what it's going to feel like to become the latest Cooney to kill another human being.

Now, my body responds to those last two words and wink face like I just watched a twenty-minute strip show.

But even as my blood rushes and my mind fills with images of Sam naked in the water, her breasts bobbing close enough to the surface for me to see her nipples pulled tight, something cold snakes up my spine from the opposite direction, warning me not to get my hopes —or my cock—up. I don't know how to be with her now.

We've been together since the rape but we haven't had sex since I *knew* about it, and I've spent a good amount of time since last summer beating myself up for not reading the signs and knowing something was wrong. I would have been so much more careful if I'd known. We could have gone slow, checked in more, made sure it was the polar opposite of what happened at that New Year's Eve party and stopped the second she felt scared or uncomfortable.

I've wondered that too—was she scared when we were together but hiding it, the way she hid so many other things?

She seemed to enjoy making love, but I don't know for sure. I don't know anything for sure except that I can't keep her waiting. I don't like the thought of her out in the jungle alone, even here on the compound where we're surrounded by a bunch of nature nerds, hippies, and health nuts more into sunset yoga than grabbing a few beers after dinner.

I meant my promise today—I'm never going to let anyone hurt her again. I'm going to stick to her like glue and be there whenever she needs me.

After changing back into my mostly dry board shorts, I tuck my cell phone and cabin key inside my pocket, grab a pair of pajama pants and a tee shirt from

Sam's bag, in case it gets cooler and she decides she'd rather walk back to the cabin in something more than a swimsuit, and head out.

I start down the trail, passing the monkeys in their tree on my way.

These three are part of a larger capuchin group that live near the waterfall where the adventure tours break for lunch. They've become so accustomed to the people on the compound that they sometimes roam close to the boundaries, looking for food. I was warned not to open my windows too wide or they'd find their way in, clean out my mini-fridge, and let themselves out through the front door. This particular species is so smart that they rub herbs on their fur for medicine and use simple objects as tools and weapons. Paola said she once watched a mother capuchin beat a snake to death with a stick to keep it away from her baby.

Animals have no moral issues with killing the predators among them. I can't say I'd enjoy being a monkey—the social structure of the white-headed capuchin sounds pretty messed up if you're anything other than an alpha male—but I envy them their moral simplicity.

And lack of law enforcement worries.

With that thought in mind, I tug my phone from my pocket, doing a Google search for American arrested in Costa Rica on drug charges while I walk. There's only a one line mention on a local news station's website, but I know the twenty-two-year-old arrested by National Police today at the airport is Scott.

One down. The easiest one, but still, the ball is in motion and once we come to a firm decision on what to do with J.D. and Jeremy, things are going to move fast.

All the way to the hot spring, my mind is churning, brainstorming and discarding various ways to get Todd's followers out to our pit without leading them there myself. But then I reach the turn off to the pool and see Sam's bikini top hanging from a limb—the sign that the spring is in use and anyone hiking by should come back later—and thoughts of anything but the woman waiting for me vanish.

I duck under the low-hanging leaves shielding the pool from the trail and tread carefully through the ferns covering the ground. I'm wearing my tennis shoes without socks instead of sandals, out of respect for the snakes that might be coming out to play now that the light is fading, but a bite on the ankle could still send me to the hospital.

Though at this point, I'd probably try to put it off for at least half an hour.

After all, what's a potentially deadly snakebite compared to the possibility of seeing Sam without her top on?

CHAPTER TWELVE

Danny

"This is the true measure of love:
when we believe that we alone can love,
that no one could ever have loved so before us,
and that no one will ever love in the same way after us."
-Goethe

I hold my breath as I round the curve in the trail and the river comes into view.

The spring fed pool is tucked into a rock formation above the riverbed, between a bluff pock-marked with mysterious looking caves and the finely pebbled bank. The runoff from the spring warms the water for several hundred feet downstream, increasing the growth rate of river algae until it looks like a dark green, underwater shag carpet.

I have to wade through a particularly slimy patch to get to the spring, slogging through the shallows in my waterlogged tennis shoes before I start the climb up the rocks. I'm halfway to the top when Sam's curly head pops up and her blue eyes peer down at me over the edge of the dark stones.

"Took you long enough," she says, grinning. "I was worried I'd be poached before you got here."

Her cheeks are flushed from the hot water, her face dewy with sweat, and her blond curls have become a fuzz ball that frizzes around her head like a cotton swab that's been through a blender. She looks wild and so stunning I stop and stare. I want to memorize everything about this moment, from the exact pink of her lips, to the glitter in her eyes, to the way she's looking at me like there is nothing else she needs to be happy.

She blinks, her smile fading as the silence stretches between us. "Is everything okay?"

I nod. "Very okay. Just stopping to admire the view."

"The view of my white girl afro?" She fluffs her curls. "It's even worse now that I'm blond."

"It's beautiful." I climb the last few feet up the rocks, bringing my face even with hers. "You're beautiful."

"You too." She leans in, pressing a gentle kiss to my lips that sends longing surging through my body, making my knees weak. "Get in. The water's amazing."

She pushes away from the rocks, drifting back to the other side of the pool, granting me my first glimpse of her body beneath the clear water. When I see the one-piece polka dot suit she's wearing, I don't know whether to be disappointed or relieved.

If Sam were naked beneath the water, I don't know if I'd be able to resist reaching for her with both hands.

"You can put the clothes and stuff on the towels,"

she says, motioning to the left side of the pool, where she's spread out three towels, side by side, flanked by whirring bug repellent lanterns. With the cushion of ferns underneath and the soft glow of the lanterns, the makeshift bed would be the perfect place to pull Sam out of the water and make love to her beneath the darkening sky.

I can't look at it without imagining Sam naked and reaching for me, so I keep my eyes on the river as I undress. I chuck off my shoes, toss my cabin key and phone onto the towels, and strip off my tee shirt before sliding into the water with a hiss.

It's hotter than I was expecting, but the heat feels good on my shoulders, which are still aching from all the paddling this afternoon, and it only takes a few seconds to adjust to the heat. When I do, I look up to find Sam watching me with an amused expression on her face.

"What?" I ask from my side of the pool.

"You left your board shorts on," she says, lips pushing into a pout.

"You have your swimsuit on," I point out, motioning toward her beneath the water. "I was following your lead."

"I only have my suit on because I didn't want to be naked if someone other than you showed up." She stands, her shoulders and breasts rising out of the water, steam swirling from her suit as the hot, damp fabric makes contact with the cooler evening air. "And I don't want you to follow my lead."

She reaches up to the tie behind her neck and slips the bow free. I watch, mesmerized as she lets the newly loose straps dangle down the front of her body and brings her hands to the top of the suit, just above the swell of her breasts.

"I want you to take the lead," she says as she draws the fabric slowly down, baring her breasts. "And take me."

My breath rushes out and my pulse pounds in my throat.

All I want to do is pull her into my arms and devour her whole. I want her tongue in my mouth and her tits in my hands. I want to pinch her nipples between my fingers, rolling them into hard points before I replace my hands with my tongue. I want to suck her into my mouth, to make love to her breasts until her body is so slick I can feel her heat on my fingers, even with the water pressing in all around us.

Instead, I force myself to stay where I am, my clenched fists at my sides. "Are you sure?"

"I'm sure." She pushes the suit lower, baring more of her irresistible skin and the taut muscles beneath. "And I don't want you to be careful or worried. All I want you to think about is what you want."

"What *I* want?" I repeat, a frown tugging at the skin between my eyes.

"Yes, what you want." She bends over, guiding the suit down her thighs and stepping free. She tosses the wad of sodden fabric onto the rocks and stands in front of me, naked and beautiful and so tempting I can barely breathe. "Which, knowing you the way I do, is probably to make me come as many times as you can before you lose control and fuck me so hard I'll ache a little when I wake up tomorrow morning."

I flinch at the thought of being rough with her.

I don't want to be like them, I don't want to do anything to remind her of the nightmare she barely survived.

I don't say a word aloud, but evidently Sam can still read my mind as well as I can read hers.

"Don't be afraid," she says, stepping closer. "If you're gentle and different and worried because of what they did, then they win, Danny. And we'll never be alone again."

My jaw clenches as I shake my head. "I don't want to hurt you. I couldn't live with myself if I—"

"You could never hurt me." She reaches out, her fingertips brushing across my chest. "You never have and you never will."

Her elegant arms twine around my neck, bringing her breasts inches from my chest, sending her summertime smell rushing through my head. I'm so hard I feel like I'm going to explode, but I keep my hands by my sides.

"I want you," she whispers, her breath warming my lips. "Don't you want me, too?"

"God, yes." I curl my hands into tighter fists, refusing to let myself reach for her until she understands exactly what she's asking for. "But if I lose control, I'm not sure I'll be able to get it back again. I haven't been with anyone in a year, Sam, and I've been so fucking lonely."

Sweat breaks out on my lip as I fight to swallow past the wave of emotion shoving up my throat. "What if, once I start, I can't stop?"

"There will be no reason to stop." She leans in, flattening her breasts against my chest. "Please, Danny, make love to me."

My control snaps and desire takes over.

By the time my mind catches up with my body, my tongue is stroking into Sam's mouth, hard and deep, and I've got her ass in my hands, drawing her tight against my aching cock. She rocks against me, making hungry sounds that make it clear she's as desperate for this as I am.

We cling to each other, bodies straining closer, fighting to escape the boundaries of our separate skins, to become us again after all the terrible time and distance. I cup her breast, rolling her nipple between my fingers and thumb, trembling as she cries out against my mouth and bites my lip.

I bite her back, dragging my teeth across her bottom lip and sucking hard as I continue to pluck at her nipple, making her moan.

A second later, she's got her hand down the front of my shorts and her fingers wrapped around my cock, stroking me hard, making my vision blur with how phenomenal it feels to have her hands on me again.

But I don't want her hands.

"Hold onto me," I gasp, head spinning as I wrap my arm around her waist and lift her out of the water. I'm out of the pool in three steps, laying Sam on the towels and shoving my shorts down my hips, so desperate to be inside her I'm shaking all over.

"Yes," she pants, hands trailing down my stomach as she reaches for my cock again. "Inside me. Please, Danny, please I—"

Her words end in a cry as I lengthen myself over her body and drive between her legs with one long stroke. I sink in, pushing through her slick heat until I'm buried inside of her. I don't think about holding back and couldn't have if I'd tried.

A floodgate has opened and all the hunger I've ignored for the past year is rushing out, demanding release, demanding I get closer, deeper, that I show Sam with every thrust of my hips that she is mine.

That she belongs to me and I belong to her and nothing is ever coming between us again.

"You're mine," I whisper, trapping her chin between my fingers as I ride her, shoving in and out of her pussy with swift, hard strokes that end with enough force to make her breasts bounce every time I drive home. "You are mine. Mine. Forever."

"Yes," she gasps, fingernails digging into my ass as she pulls me in tighter, harder. "Yes."

"And you're never leaving me again," I say, pace growing more frantic even as tears rise in my eyes.

I feel like I'm falling apart and being put back together again at the same time. My heart is falling out of my chest and into Sam's hands and all the hurt of the past year is pouring out of me with every thrust into her heat. I'm fucking her with all of it, all of the hurt and the love and the abandon only she can make me feel.

Only her. Only my Sam.

"I've missed you so much," I gasp, tears falling onto her cheeks. "I need you so much. Please don't leave me again. Please don't leave."

"I won't. I promise. I love you." She's sobbing too, clinging to me and feathering kisses over my cheeks, but we're still fucking like we're going to kill each other, like we're going to come together so hard and fast we break through to the other side of two and become one.

Heat builds low in my body, the sweet, painful pressure swelling until I'm out of my mind with it. Until I'm growling and grunting and curling my hands under Sam's back and around her shoulders so I don't fuck her straight off the towels.

Higher and higher we climb, gasping and tearing and straining toward oblivion, toward another plane where there is no past or future, there is only this moment and pleasure and my love so close.

So fucking close.

A second later, Sam calls out my name, her pussy squeezing me so tight I have no choice but to go over with her. I grit my teeth and shove my hips forward, a savage sound tearing from my throat as I come. The base of my spine is on fire and the orgasm is so intense I tremble and jerk like it's going to be the death of me, my cock pulsing inside Sam as she milks the soul right out of my body.

I don't know how much time passes, but when my body and soul finally come back together again, I'm lying heavily on top of her and she's stroking her fingers up and down my back, humming a husky song low in her throat.

"What song is that?" I ask, my voice so deep I barely recognize it.

"I don't know," she says with a soft laugh. "I didn't realize I was humming."

I pull back, bracing myself on my forearms, gazing down into her face. She's not crying anymore, but I can see the damp streaks where her tears and mine mingled on her cheeks.

"I'm sorry," I say, tracing one sad, salty trail with my finger. "I didn't know it was going to be like that."

Her lips curve on one side. "Hot as hell?"

"No, I could have guessed that." I smile, but it doesn't last for long. "I just... I didn't mean to push you to make any promises you're not ready to make."

"It's okay," she whispers, tucking my hair behind my ears. "I *am* yours. I'm sorry I forgot that for so long."

"And I'm yours," I say, throat tight. "Forever. Even if I'd never come here, Sam, even if I'd never seen you again. I know that's not how it's supposed to be, I know I'm supposed to be all right on my own...but I'm not."

Her lips tremble. "I'm not either. I'm so sorry I hurt you, babe."

"You couldn't help it. I don't blame you. I swear I don't. I just need to know that it's over now. That we're us again."

"We're us again," she says, her eyes searching mine. "I don't know why I thought we could be anything else. I'm either half of us or I'm only half alive."

My shoulders sag with relief to know that she understands and that neither of us has to be half alive anymore.

She sniffs. "I guess I'm not as smart as people think I am."

"You are very smart," I say, kissing her cheek. "It's been a hell of a year. Cut yourself some slack. And I hope you'll cut me some, too. I'm sorry that only lasted five minutes."

Her next sniff becomes a laugh. "Five minutes was plenty to get where we were going."

She pauses, biting her lip as her legs wrap tighter

around my hips. "But maybe we could try it again. A little slower this time."

My cock pulses inside of her, all too happy to oblige, but a glance around the rapidly darkening jungle proves it's past time to get back to civilization.

Reluctantly, I pull out, even though all I want is to stay balls deep in her for the rest of my life. "Let's take this back to the cabin, where we don't have to worry about getting bitten in the ass by a snake."

"All right." Sam takes my hand and lets me pull her to her feet.

I'm about to reach for my shorts, when she lunges forward, wrapping her arms around me and hugging tight. I return the embrace, dropping my head to press a kiss to the top of her head, overwhelmed by a potent mixture of love, gratitude, and fear.

This is all I want.

She's all I want and I already know I wouldn't survive losing her again.

"We're going to have to be very careful," I whisper. "This comes first. You and me. We can't let them take that away again."

She nods. "We'll be careful. We'll be quick. And then we'll be gone. Together."

My eyes slide closed and my arms tighten around her, wishing I could draw her into my body and keep her safe inside of me. Wishing that I never had to be apart from her, even for a moment.

After we make our way through the darkened trees to the cabin, we make love again, slow and sweet. I kiss every inch of her, from her freckled shoulders to the place where her pulse beats just beneath her navel to the slick flesh between her legs. She tastes like home and heaven and as she comes on my mouth, her secret, salty heat flooding across my tongue, I realize that they're the same.

And they're both Sam.

CHAPTER THIRTEEN

Sam

"Everything is hard before it is easy."
-Goethe

I had worried that letting love back into my life would dull my sharp edges, but nothing could be further from the truth.

The next morning, I wake up in Danny's arms, sore from making love until midnight, with a fire burning in my belly, more determined than ever to get blood on my hands. I lost a year of this perfect love and scarred the heart of the best person I've ever known because of Todd and his friends. It's past time for them to get what they deserve.

And then Danny and I will finally be free.

I roll over, propping my chin on his chest, watching the clear morning light creep across his face, setting his blond stubble to glowing.

With his long hair spread out across the pillow and his full lips parted in sleep, he is as beautiful as he ever was. But even at rest, he looks like a man who's been through something, who has walked through the shadows of the underworld, where the living should never have to tread. I'm the reason he knows what it's like to hurt like that, and I'm going to be the one to take his hand and lead him back into the light.

One day soon we're going to walk away from this horror and the sooner that day comes, the better.

A few minutes before seven, his eyes open. He looks disoriented for a second, but then he sees me and smiles, relief and wonder mixing on his sleepy face.

"So last night wasn't a dream," he says, hugging me closer to his warm body.

"More like a wake-up call." I kiss his scruffy cheek. "When's your last day of work again?"

He hums and his brow furrows. "I'll be back from the overnight trip Tuesday morning, but I don't have to check out of the cabin until Wednesday."

I cross my hands on his chest and prop my chin on top. "So we do all three Tuesday night and leave first thing Wednesday morning. I'll go to the airport and buy the tickets while you're busy with the training exercises today."

"Sounds like a plan." He brushes my hair from my face. "I'll give you some cash for my ticket."

"Do you care where we go?"

He shakes his head. "Nope. I've got Pete and Sean running all the tours in Porec until the end of the summer. We can go anywhere you want. Surprise me."

My breath rushes out with a mixture of terror and

anticipation. I can't wait for the morning we board that plane, even if there is still hell to go through before we get there. "I thought you'd be sick of surprises by now."

"I'm sick of being without you," he says, arm tightening around my waist. "I don't mind surprises."

"I meant what I said last night," I whisper, hoping he can hear that I mean every word. "I'm sticking with you. And from now on this comes first."

"I'm glad to hear it." He cups my bottom in his big hand, setting the aching flesh between my legs to tingling. "How are you feeling this morning?"

"Sore." I smile, before adding in a lilting voice, "But not too sore."

"Not too sore for what?" he asks, feigning innocence even as his fingers slip between my thighs, finding where I'm already slick. He bites his lip as he strokes gently in and out. "Thailand or India."

"What?" I moan as he adds a second finger, testing me, making sure I'm ready for him.

"Get us a flight to Thailand or India," he says. "Near the coastal resorts. Hotels are cheap enough there that we'll be able to shack up in a room by the beach for a month and do nothing but make love, eat curry, and swim in the ocean all day."

"Sounds like heaven," I say, sighing as he removes his fingers and rolls on top of me, spreading my thighs with a nudge of his knee that makes my desire spike fast and hot.

"No, this is heaven." He holds my gaze as he positions himself and glides slowly inside, his thickness stretching my inner walls.

The hint of soreness makes me even more aware of

how perfectly he fills me, how right it is to be joined with him like this, with nothing between us but love and skin. I wrap my arms and legs around him and give him everything, all my love, all my pain, and all my newly sprung hope for the future.

And when we're lying together after, listening to the monkeys chitter in the trees outside and bird calls echo through the jungle, I realize again what a fool I've been.

Love isn't making me soft, it's taking the weapon forged by hate and refining it in the fire Danny and I make together, transforming it into something even sharper and more deadly.

Hate gave me something worth dying for, but this is worth living for.

"Thank you," I whisper against the damp skin of his neck, where he smells like sweat and sex and Danny, a potent combination that makes me want to keep him in bed all day.

"No, thank you." He sighs. "I wish I could stay here with you all day."

I laugh. "I was just thinking that."

"Of course you were. I told you, great minds." He kisses the top of my head. "Don't go anywhere except to the airport and back, okay? I don't want you to run into any of them when I'm not around."

"All right," I say. "But we should do some recon today. What time will you be back?"

"I shouldn't be any later than two," he says, sliding his arm from beneath my shoulders and swinging his legs over the edge of the bed. "We can head over to the resort to scope things out then. I think I've figured out how to handle the J.D. and Jeremy thing without them seeing my face, but I want to roll it over in my head a little more."

I shift onto my side, propping my head up on one hand, appreciating the view as Danny gets dressed. "Want to give me a hint what you're thinking?"

He grins. "No. I want to see what you come up with while I'm gone."

"It probably won't be much," I say, wrinkling my nose. "If I haven't thought of something brilliant by now, I doubt today is going to be any different."

"Today is already different," he says, shrugging his shirt on. "You started the day with morning sex. And morning sex makes you twenty percent smarter."

My eyebrows lift. "Has that been verified by science?"

"It's been verified by my cock," he says, propping his hands on the mattress and leaning in for a kiss. "That's even better than science."

I smile against his lips. "You're right. That is better than science." I run my hand down his chest to where his shorts ride low on his hips and curl my fingers around the top of his waistband. "Are you sure you have to go this very second?"

His hand slips into my hair. "I could push it a few minutes if I skip breakfast. What did you have in mind?"

"Oh nothing, I was just thinking." I tilt my chin up, blinking innocently as I add, "If one round of morning sex is good then two ought to be even better."

He pushes me back onto the mattress. "Who needs breakfast?"

"Breakfast is for losers," I agree as our mouths meet

and I reach for the close of his shorts, already desperate to have him inside of me again.

There's no time for foreplay, but I don't need any.

I'm still wet from our first time and by the time Danny sinks into me again, fresh heat dampens my thighs, easing his way.

"God, Sam," he groans against my lips as he begins to thrust inside me. "I'm never going to get enough of you."

"Never," I agree, digging my fingers into the firm muscles of his ass, pulling him closer, deeper.

Within a few moments, we've found our rhythm and are racing toward the edge, knowing there isn't time for a slow build. But still, as his thrusts grow harder, faster, I'm right there with him, clinging to his shoulders as he tilts my hips, hitting that sweet spot deep inside that makes me crazy. He rams home again and again, his cock swelling inside of me until I know he's about to go and I can't hold on a second longer.

I bite my lip, trying to muffle the sound as I come, but my cry still echoes through the room, followed closely by Danny's deep groan of release. His cock jerks inside of me, hard enough to make me gasp and fresh waves of pleasure course from my belly out to electrify every inch of my skin.

I'm on fire and all I want to do is burn.

Burn and burn until there is nothing left among the ashes except the very core of my being, the part that has always belonged to Daniel Cooney. I've been his since I was just a kid, too young to realize that we were falling in forever love, the kind that refuses to be shut down or destroyed, no matter how scared you get, or how much you want to spare the one you love from your own suffering.

"I love you," he says, catching his breath.

"I love you, too." My heart is racing, but not from fear.

I'm not afraid anymore and my thoughts already feel less cloudy.

In fact, as I slip into my robe and grab a banana and a granola bar from my backpack for Danny, the hint of a plan is already beginning to form.

"You were right." I kiss his cheek one last time as he reaches for the door. "Today is going to be different."

"And all the days after," he promises with a certainty that makes me believe him.

CHAPTER FOURTEEN

Danny

"People who think honestly and deeply
have a hostile attitude towards the public."
-Goethe

*G*etting into The Seasons is easier than I expected, but then Sam and I have extensive pool crashing experience.

Growing up on Maui, we probably crashed every hotel pool on the island at one point or another. The secret is to dress like a tourist, act like you belong, come armed with a room number, and be prepared to play dumb if you get caught.

But we were never caught when we were kids and today is no different.

We stand up paddleboard over to the private beach in our swimsuits and by the time we've ordered smoothies from the cabana and wandered up the trail to use the showers, we're just two more guests enjoying the resort. I'm wearing my ball cap with my hair tucked underneath and Sam has her big hat and glasses on again.

She's virtually unrecognizable, but I can tell that she's still on edge. Not that I can blame her.

I don't blame her for refusing to let me come alone, either. Two sets of eyes and ears are better than one and a team effort is our best bet for getting the information we need. My computer skills aren't up to hacking The Seasons database and the front desk is never going to tell a couple of strangers a guest's room number.

The only way we're going to find out where Todd and the rest of them are staying is by lurking in the right place at the right time.

"If you need to disappear, I'll meet you by the paddleboards," I say as I get Sam settled on a bar stool in the shade not far from where the poolside waitresses pick up their drinks.

Sam tugs her straw hat lower on her face. "Okay, but you're the one who needs to be careful. I seriously doubt any of them are going to get off their lazy asses and come all the way down to the bar to get a drink when they could have someone deliver it to their lounge chair. Lie low and don't attract attention."

"I won't." I rub what I hope is a comforting hand up and down her back. "And don't worry, they aren't going to remember my face from a few pictures they saw on your phone over a year ago."

I ignore the flash of anger that follows my words.

I hate that pictures Sam took to send to *me*—private pictures of some toys she'd bought and a few racy shots of her meant to ease the loneliness of being apart for months on end—were used to paint her as some kind of deviant slut during the trial. I hate even more that those pictures might have made her a target in the first place.

Alex copped to passing Sam's phone around to Todd a few hours before the attack, but we'll never know if that's why he decided to isolate Sam in the pool room while a party raged on the other side of the building. I guess, in the end, it doesn't matter.

I don't care why Todd decided to do what he did, only that he pays for it.

"Probably not." Sam takes a deep breath, but her shoulders are still tense as they settle into place. "But be careful anyway. Text me when you've got the numbers and I'll head back to the beach."

"I will. And have a beer if you think it will help you relax a little," I say. "I know normal people can do that without wanting to drink the entire keg."

Her lips twitch. "Are you calling me normal?"

"Never," I say, leaning in to kiss her cheek. "You're the best. See you soon."

"Soon," she echoes, squeezing my hand one last time before I turn and start down the path leading to the infinity pool.

There are smaller, private pools sprinkled throughout the resort, but my gut says a bunch of fraternity boys will want to be where the people are. They'll want to see and be seen, and maybe pick up a girl or two to take out tonight.

I set up a dummy social media account months ago and I'm friends with half the SBE brothers. I know that they're pre-gaming at Guava Bar at a neighboring resort and then heading out to the club that just opened in the closest village. If Sam wasn't so insistent on me avoiding contact with the douchebags, I could probably lure them out the back door of the dance club with an offer to share a bowl and have them in my trunk a few minutes later.

But I know she wants to keep me safe, so I'm willing to play things her way.

For now.

At least until I hear the new plan she cooked up while I was out teaching people how to hang a tent from the side of a rock face. She said she wanted to wait until we had the room numbers before she fleshed out the details since those were necessary for what she had in mind.

Hopefully, before the sun starts to set, I'll have what we need. I can't imagine frat boys will wait much more than an hour between drinks, not when they're on vacation and pounding beers is basically the sole reason for joining a frat in the first place.

I pause in the shade near the towel return, scanning the pool deck as I finish my drink. The frat boys are, as I suspected, easy to find.

About twenty pasty, recently graduated college kids with the beginnings of scorched shoulders are loudly holding court at the opposite end of the pool. Someone brought out speakers they've attached to one of their iPhones and they are thoughtlessly subjecting the rest of the guests to Bob Marley played loud enough to be heard over the waterfall feature streaming from the second floor of the resort.

I spot J.D. and Jeremy near the speakers, their nearly

identical dark brown haircuts damp from the pool, laughing with a much bigger guy I don't recognize. Todd has his back turned to me, but I've looked at his picture enough in the past year to memorize the exact fall of his stupid, Justin Bieber circa 2010 haircut from any angle. He's in the pool, his arms draped back across the concrete behind him and a half-empty beer in one hand, talking to two girls in barely-there bikinis who have no idea the man they're flirting with is a monster.

A part of me wants to wait until the women move away from Todd and warn them to stay the hell away from him, but I can't afford to attract attention and there's no guarantee they'd believe me. I'm four inches taller and a good fifty pounds heavier than Todd. On the surface, I'm probably more imposing and most people don't stop to look below the surface, a fact I'm grateful for as I grab a towel from the attendant—who doesn't even bother to write down the room number I mumble beneath my breath—and aim myself toward the other side of the pool.

I find a free lounge chair close enough to pick out the details of various conversations, but hopefully not close enough to get on anyone's radar, and settle in. I spread out my towel, strip off my tee shirt, and stretch out on the chair with my phone in my lap and my head tilted down. I open a book in my Kindle app and pretend to be reading, but I'm really just swiping my thumb every few seconds and waiting for one of these bastards to order more beer.

While I wait, I try to zone out and not think too much about anything else I'm overhearing. If I listen too closely to these fucks going about their lives like they deserve to be free and soaking in a pool at a seven hundred dollar per night resort, I might lose control and strangle them right here.

It was clear from my first glimpse of the SBE brothers at the airport that none of Sam's attackers are plagued by guilt over what they did. But seeing them in their element, acting like the world exists only to facilitate their pleasure, talking to the staff waiting on them like shit and leaving their empty cups littered across the pool deck instead of taking the five steps to the trash can, makes me sick to my stomach.

The coldest part of me wants to kill them all, wipe out the entire frat before any of these arrogant, careless, greedy trust fund babies can pass on their worthless genes to another generation.

But that's the difference between someone like Todd and someone like me.

I don't give my monster free reign.

My monster will only be allowed out of its cage for one night and only one life will be lost. *His.*

I glance up in time to see Todd lifting his hand to the waitress on the other side of the pool and to hear him insult the size of her ass when it takes her longer than he would prefer for her to make her way through the crowd. The two girls laugh at his joke and cast nasty looks at the other woman as she squats down beside the water to take Todd's order, eyeing her perfectly healthy-sized backside like it's an offense to their sense of decency.

I decide right then that they deserve Todd Winslow, after all.

"I'll take another Corona and bring two mai tais for

my friends." Todd flicks his empty can in the waitress's direction while she tries to write down his order and clean up his mess at the same time. "And make sure the drinks are cold this time. I'm not paying ten dollars for hot beer."

"Thank you, sir," the waitress says in a resigned voice that makes it clear she's used to dealing with assholes like this on a daily basis. "Room number?"

"The Rosa Blanca suite," Todd says with a sigh. "Third time."

"Of course. Be right back." The waitress stands and hurries away toward the bar.

Todd rolls his eyes, making his audience of two giggle. One girl shakes her head and insists that laziness is the reason people from third world countries lag behind the rest of the world.

Like most idiots, she doesn't realize that the U.S. is practically a third world country, the divide between the haves and have-nots has grown so vast. And if the rich keeping getting tax breaks and the U.S. continues to be the *only* developed country that doesn't ensure its citizens have health care, soon we'll be slipping even further behind the rest of the world. After all, there are already counties in the American South with lower life expectancies than Bangladesh. I know. I used to live in one of them.

Ignoring the chatter of the entitled and clueless, I grit my teeth and turn back to my phone, making a note that Todd is in the Rosa Blanca suite though I know I won't forget.

I won't forget a moment of this afternoon.

There's something intimate about knowing you're

going to kill someone, something that makes me hyper aware of Todd's every movement, his every breath. My commitment to destroying him makes me feel weirdly connected to the man and I hate him for that, too. I don't want to feel connected to the person who nearly destroyed the woman I love. I just want him to be gone.

By the time I finally get room numbers for J.D. and Jeremy—rooms 2012 and 2015 respectively—I'm sick to my stomach. I would blame the smoothie, but food poisoning takes longer to take effect.

The knot in my gut is all thanks to the Sigma Beta Epsilon brothers.

Tucking my phone back into my pocket, I grab my shirt and towel and start back toward the towel desk. I'm nearly to the far side of the pool when a prickling feeling between my shoulder blades makes me pause and glance back over my shoulder to find Todd Winslow watching me walk away.

My sunglasses are completely reflective. There's no way he can see my eyes, but for some reason I can't shake the feeling that he's staring right at me.

I pause, glancing at the clock set into the bricks beside the tours and activities desk on the other side of the pool, then check my phone, pretending there was some valid reason for looking back aside from the fact that my lizard brain sensed I'd attracted a predator's attention. As I turn again, I risk a glance Todd's way to find him once again focused on the two increasingly wasted girls he's been flirting with for the past hour.

A part of me insists the moment of eye contact was just a coincidence, but another part of me thinks Todd is as aware of me as I am of him.

I toss my used towel into the bin but leave my tee shirt off, hoping the cool air coming off the water will help relieve the nausea making my stomach pulse beneath my ribs. By the time I get back to Sam, I'm feeling better and have convinced myself that I don't have to say anything to her about that one uncomfortable moment.

Todd was so wrapped up in himself he hadn't noticed me the entire time I was eavesdropping on his conversation. It must have been the sudden movement that caught his eye. He would have glanced up no matter who got up from their lounge chair and walked away. The look meant nothing. He didn't recognize me; he isn't suspicious.

Everything is fine, or as fine as it can be considering the circumstances.

As I hug Sam close and whisper, "I've got everything we need," I believe it. I believe because it's what I want to believe and because I've mistaken Todd's lack of guilt for a belief in his own innocence.

Those two things can look the same from the outside, but they aren't.

A man who believes he's innocent isn't looking over his shoulder. A man who knows he's guilty, but doesn't give a shit, sleeps with one eye open, determined that someone else will always pay the price for his sins.

Later I would look back and understand the distinction, but right now I'm still innocent enough to walk down to the beach with my arm around Sam, thinking no mistakes have been made.

CHAPTER FIFTEEN

Sam

"Knowing is not enough; we must apply.
Willing is not enough; we must do."
-Goethe

*H*iring a prostitute is a lot easier than buying a gun or a kilo of cocaine.

And neither of those were a real strain, considering I have virtually no experience with the criminal element.

I wanted to meet with the woman we tracked down through a dating app—my Spanish is better than Danny's and I didn't want her to be freaked out by meeting someone as large as Danny in a dark alley. But he said she was more likely to remember the details of being hired by a woman than a man and I had to admit he was right.

So I prepped him in advance and kept my phone in my lap while he went to the meeting, just in case he needed help answering any of the woman's questions. Turns out, her English was probably better than my Spanish and she and Danny had all the details of the "surprise" for his buddies worked out in ten minutes.

Late Tuesday afternoon, Danny will meet her near the market, pay half her fee, and drop her off at The Seasons. From there, she'll call up to J.D.'s and Jeremy's rooms and guide them to the location of the private party, allegedly organized by their friend "Todd", the name Danny gave her when they met. She assumes she'll be meeting Todd and a couple of other prostitutes at the small house we've rented for the night, where they'll party and she'll receive the other half of her fee.

Instead, Danny and I will be waiting with masks on just inside the door.

I'm in charge of knocking the woman out with a choke hold and then dosing her with enough ketamine to keep her knocked out for an hour or so; Danny's in charge of knocking the men out, administering their dose of the knockout drug, and getting them into the trunk of the rental car.

From there, our paths will diverge. Danny will take J.D. and Jeremy out to the pit he's dug in the jungle, and I'll take Rosa back to her apartment, where I'll leave her with the other half of her money.

"That's it," Danny says, leaning forward to write down the number of Rosa's apartment building. "Four-teen twenty-three."

We've been following Rosa—or whatever her real name is—for over three hours. From the alley where she met with Danny, to a swanky hotel where she went upstairs with a man twice her age, to the market where she bought milk, fresh fruit, and tampons, and now to this crumbling apartment building near the southern edge of Liberia.

"This is good." I study the entrance as Danny and I walk by, the hoods of our sweatshirts pulled up against the cool wind. The temperature dropped suddenly tonight and though it's still in the high sixties, it feels cool after eighty-degree days. "There's a lobby with a sofa in front of the mailboxes. She should be safe there until she wakes up, with two locked doors between her and the street."

"Are you going to be able to carry her in?" Danny asks. "Even if you park close, there are ten steps up to the lobby."

I make a scoffing noise. "She's about as big around as my thigh. I think I'll manage."

"She is tiny." He puts his arm around my waist with a sigh. "I feel bad for her. I know there's nothing we can do, but..."

"I know." I lean into him as we turn the corner, starting back toward the well-lit streets of the Centro where we parked the car. "I would say that maybe being drugged will give her a wake-up call that it's time to find other work, but it's not like prostitution is any woman's first choice. I'm sure she doesn't feel like she has other options or she wouldn't be selling herself."

"Is this fucked up?" Danny asks, his voice low. "Feeling bad for a prostitute when we're planning to kill a man?"

I consider the question, a faint niggle of guilt tugging at the back of my mind. "I don't know. Maybe. But I don't think right and wrong are as simple as some people would have you believe."

"Sounds like something my sister would say."

"I wish I knew her better," I say. "I remember what you said last summer, about her and Gabe still stealing things. Do you know why?"

He shrugs. "We've never talked about it, but I think it's their way of feeling like they're giving back. They both have a Robin Hood complex, always looking out for the underdog."

"Stealing from the rich and giving to the poor?"

"Something like that," he says, before continuing in a wry tone. "But it's part entertainment, too. I think they get off on the rush of breaking the law and not getting caught."

I blink, surprised. "Wow...that's... I don't know. I'd rather go surfing."

"Me too," he says with a laugh. "Or mountain-biking or cliff camping. That's my idea of a rush."

His smile fades as he shoves his hoodie off his head with one big hand. "I never thought I'd be like them. Not that I judge them or think I'm better than they are or anything. I just...didn't see myself going that way."

My throat tightens, but I don't pull away. I'm learning not to run, even when being close scares me. "Do you think you'll resent me someday? When it's all over and you've had time to regret everything we're doing?"

"Never," he answers immediately.

"You're sure?"

"Positive." His fingers curl into my shoulder. "I've always known the world isn't fair, but this goes so far beyond unfair. They're criminals, and criminals shouldn't be able to hurt people and walk away without a mark on them. That's what I believe and I'm not going to regret standing up for it. Or for you."

We both fall quiet, Danny holding me close to his side as he scans the street, watchful for potential threats. I wonder if he's thinking about that night in Auckland, when we were almost mugged.

No matter how dangerous it was, I'm glad I fought back. I never want to be a victim again.

But I don't want to be one of the bad guys, either.

"Should we call Rosa and cancel?" I stop in the middle of the sidewalk, turning to face Danny in the dim light of the flickering street lamp at the end of the block.

"No! Why?" His brow furrows. "I'm just talking, Sam. I'm not second-guessing the plan. It's solid. Way better than mine. This way, J.D. and Jeremy never see our faces and the only person who can connect us to them is a prostitute who isn't going to want to talk to the police."

"I know, but what if I hurt her?" I ask. "What if she has a bad reaction to the drug? Or what if she slips out of the chokehold and I have to fight her? I could end up breaking her nose or—"

"You're not going to break her nose," Danny says. "You know what you're doing and the ketamine will keep her out. And she's not going to expect you to be grabbing her from behind. She'll be out before she has a chance to fight back."

"But there is a chance something will go wrong and she'll pay the price for it," I insist. "That's the reality. I'm justifying hurting this woman because someone hurt me. I'm sure that kid who tried to mug us last summer was doing the same thing. Someone hurt him and so he decided to hurt us and take what he needed to survive."

Danny shakes his head. "It's not the same thing, Sam."

"It's close enough. Maybe too close." I close my eyes, pinching the aching places at the backs of my lids together with my finger and thumb. "I don't know. I don't know where to draw the line anymore."

"And that's okay. That's why I'm here," he says, fingers circling my wrist, tugging my hand away from my eye sockets and giving it a gentle shake. "Look at me."

I open my eyes and look up into his shadowed face.

"This isn't going to be easy. Breaking the rules never is," he says. "But that doesn't mean some of them don't need to be broken. J.D. and Jeremy need to be taught a lesson. And Todd has to die. If he lives, you know he's going to hurt someone else, a hell of a lot worse than you'll hurt Rosa. He'll probably hurt a lot of people."

"I know." I nod, swallowing past the lump in my throat.

"There's only one reason to change the plan," Danny says. "And that's if you think you're going to be exchanging one thing that will eat you alive for another. That's what Caitlin said to me when I first started talking about revenge. She didn't tell me not to, just not to get caught, and not to do it if I couldn't walk away from it after and find a way to be happy."

I lift my hands to Danny's chest, letting them rest there, feeling his muscles strong and solid beneath my palms. "Until that night at the hot spring... I didn't think I remembered how to be happy."

"I know." He covers my hands with his, warming my cool fingers. "So maybe things have changed now. That's okay, too. It's okay to change your mind. I'm with you, no matter what you decide. I'm going to be fine either way, as long as I know we're together."

We stand in silence, but I can't concentrate on anything except the feel of his heartbeat pulsing steadily beneath my fingertips.

Precious heart. Precious chest.

Can I put them in more danger? No matter how solid the plan or how much I need to see justice done? Does it take more strength to follow through with what I've started or to walk away?

Maybe Danny and I can be free without this. Maybe all I have to do is let go and give myself permission to be happy again.

Happy, while the man who looked you in the eyes and smiled while men raped you goes free, using this easy escape as a reason to believe he is above the law.

Untouchable.

Unstoppable.

And the next time he hurts someone, her blood will be on your hands as much as his.

"I don't know," I whisper. "I don't know what to do."

"Then we don't do anything." He takes my hand in his and squeezes tight. "We'll let things stand for now. We've got three more days. Come Tuesday morning, if you've changed your mind, we can call things off with Rosa then. You don't have to decide right now. Midnight decisions are never a good idea anyway."

I glance sharply up at him, eyes widening. "You're kidding me. It's not midnight."

"Not kidding." He slips his phone from his pocket and hits the button, illuminating the screen showing that's it's nearly a quarter after twelve. "And I told Paola I'd help her lead the first zip line tour tomorrow since Henri pulled his shoulder. We should head back."

"All right." Holding on to his hand, we set a faster clip through the Centro and back to the car. We don't talk much on the way back to the cabin or while getting ready for bed.

But when we're beneath the covers, Danny turns to me and pulls me into his arms, whispering, "Whatever you decide, Sam. Really. There will never be any judgment from me, either way."

And then he makes love to me with an honesty that makes me believe him. But even though it feels so right to be in his arms and I know he's telling the truth, I keep thinking back to the things he said last summer when we were on the verge of falling apart, when he made it clear he rises or falls according to my lead.

Last year, I tumbled off the pedestal he'd put me on and dragged him down with me. He fell off the wagon and had been ready to break important promises he'd made to his family all because I'd failed to be the hero he'd thought I was.

I know it's not right to expect myself to be strong and good for two people, but what's right and what's true are rarely the same thing.

Danny and I have already admitted that we aren't whole without each other. Maybe we'll always be that way. Maybe falling in love so young and making forever promises when we had no idea how long forever could be has crippled us as individuals. Alone, we probably aren't what psychiatrists would consider stable, but together we are solid, unstoppable.

But it has almost always been my job to put on the brakes, to decide whether we should use our unstoppable energy for good or to call a time out when we're getting close to doing something we shouldn't. I wasn't up to the job last year and I'm not sure I'm up to it now.

I only know that I love him, this man who wraps his arm around my waist and curls his strong body into mine with an intensity that makes it clear he'd shelter me from every hurt in the world if he could. He is our heart. I am our conscience. And if I don't want to put both of us at risk again, I need to start doing my job.

I need to decide what's more important—revenge or the safety of the man I love—and I have to decide quickly.

The clock is ticking and lives hang in the balance. Not just Todd's life, or J.D.'s or Jeremy's, but mine and Danny's and the lives of the people who love us, who will suffer the aftershocks of the decisions we make.

Decisions that once made can never be unmade, no matter how many nights I lie in the dark, staring up at the ceiling, wondering if I should have done things differently.

CHAPTER SIXTEEN

Danny

*"Nothing shows a man's character
more than what he laughs at."*
-Goethe

I can tell the question of what to do with the SBE brothers is weighing on Sam in a way it wasn't before, but I'm not going to try to talk to her about it again.

No matter how much I love her or hate the men who hurt her, my opinion doesn't matter. This is her war. She has to make the final call and give the marching orders. And if she says we walk away, I'll walk away, no matter how much I want to punish those assholes or how much they deserve it.

If Sam doesn't think she'll be able to live with herself after, I will take her hand, get on the plane to Thailand, and do my best to forget about the men who stole a year of our lives together, forget that they are still out there, living a life without scars or consequences.

I'm a different person than I was a year ago.

I still want to do the right thing, but more importantly, I want to do the right thing for Sam. Nothing is more important than that. I let her down once by being too focused on an ideal instead of the woman I love. I won't make the same mistake again.

*S*aturday morning, I ease out of bed quietly, figuring at least Sam should be able to sleep in after the late night. I dress quickly and tuck my toothbrush into my bag so I can go straight from the mess hall to the visitor center after breakfast.

On my way out, I pause at the door, looking back at the bed.

Sam is curled on her side with one arm tucked under her pillow, her lighter hair making the smattering of freckles on her nose stand out more than they did before. With the freckles and her face soft with sleep, she looks so much younger. She could be fourteen, thirteen, that same girl in the fluffy black dress and combat boots who cared enough about the new kid to step in and speak up when I was about to get my ass kicked.

She's always been a good person. I'm not surprised that she's reached a crossroads with her own conscience now that the time to act is so close. I just hope she understands that I meant what I said last night. I'm not going to judge her, either way. If she wants to walk, I'll walk. And if she needs vengeance, I'll help her take it. I would take it for her if she would let me, but she's always been one to fight her own battles, even when she was a little girl standing up to bullies twice her size.

My heart turns over, my chest aching with love so fierce it feels like it might tear me apart.

I'm tempted to cross to the bed and kiss her awake, just to hear her say goodbye, but instead I shut the door and start toward the mess hall. She needs rest if she's going to look all the hard questions in the face and find answers and I have to get food in my belly and my tired ass ready for work.

As I cross the hard-packed ground, the air around me is filling with the sounds of the compound coming to life. But gently, the people and animals and the sounds of both starting their days in harmony with each other. This is a special place, so unspoiled that I can't help wishing Sam and I were here just to enjoy the peace.

This is a place where Nature rules and though she isn't always kind, she at least gives you a fighting chance. Nature doesn't believe in inequality. The weaker animals have superior numbers and adaptations to protect them, and the stronger animals have to fight to survive every bit as much as the creatures they prey upon. There's harmony in that and in the way these people have carved out an existence from the jungle without disturbing the natural order.

It's easy to find your center here, and by the time I've had coffee and eggs with rice, I'm looking forward to a day outside in the sun, enjoying the simple things.

But I should have known better than to drop my guard.

It's a small world, especially this corner of it, and no red-blooded American frat boy can resist the call of an

Extreme Zip Line. Still, when I jump out of Paola's jeep at the visitor center to find the entire Sigma Beta Epsilon frat sprawled across the benches outside the office and spilling down the front steps, I can't believe my shit luck.

But there they are—J.D., Jeremy, and Todd, who is already hitting on a pretty, way-too-young-for-him blond girl in a black tank top. He's wearing a faded orange tee shirt and that smug look that makes me want to punch him in the mouth a few hundred times.

My gut screams for me to get out of here, but I can't. If I play sick, Paola won't be able to get anyone else here in time to help her lead the tour.

Besides, Todd has already spotted me.

As I climb the steps behind Paola to grab the manifest and make sure the waivers have all been signed, I can feel his eyes on me. There's no question now. He recognizes me—either from the pool or the pictures on Sam's phone. If it's the first, I can play it off and say that I have friends at the resort who let me come use the pool on my days off.

But if it's the second...

I force a smile for Paola as she makes a joke about the amount of testosterone on the tour today—aside from the girl Todd is flirting with, who's here with her parents and younger brother, there are only two other women—but inside I'm making plans.

There are fifteen different zip lines and the platforms in the middle of the tour are over two hundred feet in the air. We're strapped in at all times—either to a platform or the zip line—but if someone were to accidentally become detached, stumble, and take a fall off one of those bigger platforms, it would be deadly. It's happened before at other zip lines. That's why everyone on these tours is required to sign a waiver acknowledging that they won't hold the company responsible if they're seriously injured or even killed.

If Todd recognizes me as Sam's boyfriend, it will no longer be a matter of what she wants. The decision will be out of her hands. I'll have to take care of him today.

Todd is a monster, but he's not an idiot. He'll realize it's no coincidence that the boyfriend of the woman he raped is in a tiny vacation town in Costa Rica the exact same week that he is. He'll suspect something and he's not the type to consider all the options before he acts. He'll take steps to neutralize the threat to his safety and if I'm not careful, I could be the one taking a fall.

I'm going to have to keep a close eye on him, all while pretending to be fine and keeping a bunch of hungover frat boys from getting hurt in the process.

The thought obliterates the last of my Zen.

The beer fumes rising off the group are so potent I'm pretty sure it's a violation of my sobriety to breathe the air around them for too long. It makes me feel sorry for the six people on the tour who weren't up all night chugging beer.

As Paola and I gather the group of twenty-five together at the trailhead and she starts briefing them on the safety procedures, I notice the family of four and the two German women are careful to stay at the far edge of the press of stinking bodies. I'm disgusted on their behalf.

The privileged, American, twenty-something male is an embarrassment to our country. I exempt myself from the group by virtue of the fact that I've lived in Croatia since I was thirteen, and though my sister married into money she used to finish raising me, I started my life in the gutter. And the marks of the gutter never truly leave you.

A part of me is still that feral little shit who learned to scare the bullies away by hitting harder than any of the other runts. He will always be with me, like my damaged molars, a result of childhood tooth decay fucking up my adult teeth. Before Caitlin took over as my surrogate mother, worked her ass off to afford trips to the dentist, and forced my ungrateful ass to brush, no one cared if I went to bed dirty with teeth that hadn't been cleaned in a week.

My inner hood rat is awake and watchful now. Even as I smile and introduce myself, seeming to scan the entire group in front of me, my focus is on Todd, waiting for him to confirm that he's a threat. I remember the violent lessons of my early childhood well. Destroy or be destroyed, throw the first punch or wish you had when you end up in the hospital pissing blood because the guy who got the jump on you damaged your kidneys.

Those lessons had begun to fade from my conscious mind, but the past year has brought them all back to the surface, where they're going to stay. I won't make the mistake of believing in the end of hard times or happily ever after again.

No matter how much I wish the world were a safe place for good people, it isn't.

It isn't enough to do your best, love your fellow man, and try to do no harm. Sometimes you have to be ready to fight back, and fight dirty because the one thing you can be sure of is that the bad guys never play fair.

"Any questions?" Paola asks in her strange little accent that has half the frat boys smirking at each other beneath their ball caps.

Paola is petite, with long dark hair she wears pulled back in a ponytail, big brown eyes, and a perpetually friendly expression on her makeup-free face. She's more cute than sexy, but I guess the accent is enough to get the SBE brothers going.

Great, another thing to add to my list: keep an eye on Paola.

She's wiry and a lot tougher than she looks, but she shouldn't have to defend herself from sexual harassment while she's at work. If these booze-soaked losers step over the line, I'll make sure they know to take a step back.

"All right, if there are no questions, then let's get started! It's going to be a beautiful day." Paola grins and turns to lead the way up the trail to the first zip line platform.

I hang back, waiting for the rest of the tour to fall in behind her before I follow up from the rear. On his way by, Todd smiles and nods his head in my direction. "What's up, man? You always let the lady do the talking?"

I grin and stretch lazily, forcing myself to act like I don't want to smash his head against the nearest rock until it explodes. "She's better at it than I am," I drawl. "Especially this early in the morning. If I were on vacation, I'd still be asleep, dude."

He laughs. "Yeah, I had to drag half these assholes

out of bed this morning. Some people have to be forced into a good time."

I tell myself he's not talking about Sam and what he bullied the rest of his friends into doing to her. I tell myself I can't lose control three fucking steps into the hike. I tell myself that if I break now I will have tipped my hand and Todd will have the advantage from here on out.

In the five seconds it takes to form my reply, I tell myself a lot of smart things, but it still takes all the self-control I possess to force another smile and say, "I hear ya. But it's great out here. Your friends are going to have a blast."

"No doubt, man," he says, his eyes narrowing on my face for a second before he turns and starts up the trail.

I notice that he's managed to fall in right behind the girl he was talking to when I drove up—the girl who is here with her family and probably no more than sixteen years old. I wonder if that was the reason for our conversation. Maybe he was just stalling to get closer to the girl.

Or maybe he intended every word to be a double-edged sword shoved straight into my gut.

I don't know, but the brief interaction puts me even more on edge.

CHAPTER SEVENTEEN

Danny

*A*ll the way up to the first platform, I'm replaying every word and fighting the wave of sickness that sends my breakfast gurgling back up my throat.

I can't believe I spoke to him. I can't believe I smiled at the man who raped my girlfriend.

The jungle blurs and in my mind I see his hands on her, keep imagining that smug smile on his face while he filmed his friends taking turns. It's all I can do not to rush him, tackle him to the ground, and beat him until he's nothing but a bloody stain on the forest floor.

It shouldn't have to be this way. I shouldn't have to hide my rage and hate. I should be able to throw my knowledge of what he's done in his face and challenge him to a fight to the death. Right here, right now.

Civilization has gone too far. Yes, we should feed the hungry and heal the sick. Yes, we should have equal rights and equal pay and an end to discrimination for the color of your skin or who you choose to love. But we should bring back the duel. I should be able to call Todd out and fight him with swords or guns or fists.

I should be able to kill him for what he's done.

It is my right as someone who loves the person he nearly destroyed.

We coast down the first zip line and press higher into the mountains. The sun is shining brightly, but a cool breeze stirs the canopy, keeping the humidity at bay. It's the nicest day since I arrived in Costa Rica, but I might as well be in hell.

As I follow the three men who attacked Sam deeper into the jungle, I slowly start to lose my shit. I try to smile and joke with the other guys as I strap them in and pretend this is just another tour, like the hundreds of others I've led for my company in Croatia and others across Europe, but inside I'm dying. I can feel my temperature spiking and my stomach churning like I just chugged a bottle full of acid instead of vitamin water.

The stress of keeping everything I'm feeling locked inside is making me physically ill. Sweat pours down my face and my hands shake as I double check the shorter German woman's harness, which she said felt loose on the last ride. She smiles and thanks me after, but shoots me a look that makes it clear I look as shitty as I feel.

As she walks away, taking her place in the lineup for the third zip line, Paola—who is about to climb the platform—pauses and reverses direction, coming to stand beside me.

"You don't look so good, Danny. Are you okay?" She tries to lay the back of her hand on my forehead, but I step away.

"You don't want to touch me, P," I say, with a shaky laugh. "I'm sweating like a pig."

She frowns. "I can see. Michael said there's something going around from the cruise ship that landed a few days ago. A nasty virus or something. Maybe you've caught it. Do we need to turn around?"

I shake my head.

'm not turning around. I don't want to give the brothers any more reason to remember me and I still need to figure out if Todd's playing games or if he thinks I'm just a tour guide. "Nah, I'll be fine. I think it's something I ate last night. I'll push through."

"All right, but why don't you take a few minutes to yourself once we get the last of them on the line," she says. "I'm going to take the group up to the waterfall for a rest and posing for pictures. You can rejoin us on the trail on the way down. That will spare you a mile of hiking."

"Thanks," I say, knowing I need the time to pull myself together, but hating to leave Paola alone with this crew. "Don't take any shit from the jocks, okay? And radio if you need help. I can be there in five minutes."

Her dark eyes flash as she smiles. "Don't worry about me, hero. I can handle myself."

She pats me affectionately on the back and starts toward the platform, having no idea she's out in the middle of nowhere with three men who would be in prison right now if justice had been served.

I mop the sweat from my face with the bottom of my shirt, force a smile, and somehow manage to get all twenty-five people sent down the zip line without tossing any of the SBE brothers off the edge of the platform.

If an "accident" happens, it's going to have to be when Todd and I are alone, and we haven't reached the highest lines yet. This platform is only a hundred feet off the ground. That's potentially survivable, and if I send the guy flying, I want to make sure he's never going to be getting up after he hits the ground.

Once I'm alone, I sit down in the shade and close my eyes, centering myself, pushing away all the emotions tying my body in knots.

There is a time and a place for passion, but this isn't it. I need to be calm, calculating, in control. If Sam can hold it together while she's in the same space with these guys, I can, too. They've ripped my world apart, but they've never laid hands on me, and if they did, I'm strong enough to take on all three of them and come out on top. No matter how far women have come in the past century, it's still far safer to be a man.

It makes me hope Sam and I have boys just so I don't have to feel so damned scared for my kids all the time.

Just a few days ago, I was sure the dream of a family with Sam was dead and buried. But now, I can see a glimmer of hope in the future. Someday, when all this is over and Sam and I have both had time to heal, we'll be settled and happy together. And eventually that happiness will get so big we'll be ready to share it with someone else, someone who's half her and half me and who we'll love enough to make up for all the horrible things in the world.

We just have to make it to Wednesday morning and get on that plane and all things will be possible.

Focusing on the future, on that not-too-distant time when Todd will cease to exist for me and Sam, helps me ground myself. It doesn't matter if he's dead or just somewhere far, far away, he'll only be a problem for three more days and I can do anything for three days. If I made it an entire year without knowing if I'd ever see Sam again—or if she were even alive—I can do this with one eye closed and my arms tied behind my back.

I pound a handful of almonds from my backpack, willing my stomach to settle, and wash them down with another swig of water.

By the time I hitch myself to the zip line, I'm nearly back to normal.

I take the ride, managing to enjoy the rush of the wind cooling my skin and the vibrant, wild, alive smell of the jungle rising up around me. At the end of the line, I trot down the steps and start up the trail toward the waterfall, knowing I'll have time to catch them before they leave. I don't feel like I need a rest anymore. I want to keep moving, keep my blood pumping and my body ready to respond at a moment's notice. I'm not going to think, I'm going to act and trust that my gut will lead me in the right direction.

Halfway up the trail, I hear soft voices coming from off the trail ahead and slow down. It's a male voice and a female voice, but too quiet for me to place who's speaking. I'm guessing that maybe it's the husband and wife from the group, taking a private moment, but when I get a visual through the leaves, I see Todd and the blond girl.

I freeze, my boots making a scratching noise in the

underbrush as I stop, but neither of them seems to notice.

The girl is leaning back against a wide tree trunk, looking up at Todd with a mixture of horror and disbelief as he says something I can't make out. His back is to me and he has one arm braced on the tree above the girl's head. But it's his other hand that attracts my attention.

I watch as he reaches up, pinching the girl's nipple through her tank top and twisting with a roughness that makes her cry out and cringe away from him. But he holds tight, whispering beneath his breath until her cry becomes an almost inaudible whimper.

I don't know what he's said to her, but whatever it was, it convinces her to stand still and silent while he reaches a hand up her shirt and pinches her again, this time, skin on skin. She grimaces and squeezes her eyes shut, but doesn't fight him. I don't know why she doesn't fight—there are people close enough to hear her call out and come to help her—but she's so young and Todd is an experienced monster. Making a victim of an innocent kid is no doubt easy for him. He probably didn't even have to try.

If I'd seen something like this even fifteen minutes ago, I wouldn't have been able to stop myself from running to help the girl. But I'm colder now, working from a place of thought, not feeling.

And so I watch as Todd shoves her shirt up, baring her small breasts and the faint bruises already forming on her nipples. I watch as he pulls his dick out and jerks himself off to the sound of the girl's whimpers, all while inflicting more pain with his free hand. Near the end, he twists her sensitive flesh so hard that she falls to the ground with a guttural sound of pain.

The moment her knees hit the earth, he comes, splashing the sticky fluid onto one of her tear-streaked cheeks.

Everything is quiet for a moment after, like the forest is holding its breath in silent disapproval of what's happened, and then Todd laughs.

He *laughs* and tosses a napkin from his pocket onto the ground in front of the girl as he takes a step back.

"Clean up and come join the group," he says. "But give me a head start. We don't want to be seen together, do we? Then your dad might figure out what a slut you are."

I barely have time to crouch down, hiding beneath the wide, green leaves of one of the giant ferns growing beside the trail, before Todd turns and starts toward me. He emerges onto the trail, not five feet from where I'm squatting, but he turns the other way, strolling back up toward the waterfall like he doesn't have a care in the world.

But then, he probably doesn't.

He doesn't have any regrets, he doesn't have a conscience, and the world will be a more dangerous place as long as he's in it.

As I watch the girl stumble after him a few minutes later, swiping the tears from her cheeks and tightening her ponytail with trembling hands, I silently tell her I'm sorry. I shouldn't have had to see what just happened to know what needed to be done, but I did. And now there is no more doubt in my mind.

But I'm not going to do it here.

I was wrong about being on Todd's radar—it was the girl he was focused on—and he deserves worse than a swift, relatively painless death. He deserves to know exactly why he's being put down, to have time to dread what's coming next, and then to die knowing he's not the biggest, baddest motherfucker in the jungle and that his life is over and nothing he did was worth a shit.

I'm going to get through this tour, tell Sam what happened, and let her know I no longer have any choice about what to do with Todd. I'm going to kill him. For Sam, for that kid who was lured into the woods by a good-looking older guy and ended up meeting a wolf instead of a prince, and for all the women Todd won't live to hurt. He is a disease that infects everything he touches and he has to be stopped.

I haven't felt called to do many things in my life— aside from loving Sam and taking care of my crazy family —but I feel called to do this. The sense that destiny is on my side for once floods through me, drawing me even more firmly to my center, focusing my thoughts on what needs to be done.

I backtrack down the trail and take the shortcut, meeting Paola and the rest of the group as they come around the loop and start toward the next zip line.

"You look better," she says, chucking me on the arm.

"I feel better." I smile as Todd walks by on her other side, surrounded by his brothers, all of them laughing as they give one of the guys shit for pissing on his shoes when he went into the jungle near the waterfall.

And I do feel better.

Because I know he won't be laughing for long.

CHAPTER EIGHTEEN

Sam

*"At the moment of commitment
the entire universe conspires to assist you."*
-Goethe

*D*anny and I sit on the beach, watching the sunset, the story he's just finished hovering in the air around us.

I feel it settling on my skin, sinking into my bones, washing away the last of my doubt. Finally, my conscience relaxes back into the shadowy corners it has inhabited for the past year with a wave of its hand, giving its blessing to murder.

"We need to decide how to do it," I say, stretching my legs out on the warm, powdery sand. "His suite is on the edge of the property. There's a chance no one would hear a gunshot."

"But there's a chance they would," Danny says.

"What about poison? I could make sure he's alone and bribe a maid to deliver a bottle laced with something to his room."

"What if he calls for help?"

"I force my way into the suite after the maid is gone and make sure he doesn't," he says. "I don't mind sitting on his chest and making sure he stays put until he's dead."

I shiver though the wind is warmer tonight than last night. "I know this is right, but...it's still hard. Hearing you talk like that."

He takes my hand, curling his fingers around mine. "You know what I've been thinking about a lot lately?"

"What?" I ask, leaning my head on his shoulder.

"Destiny. Fate. Whatever you want to call it. Things that are meant to be." He pauses, stretching his legs out beside mine, the coarse hairs on his calves brushing against my smooth ones. "But I think destiny is just the word people give to a decision that couldn't be made any other way. You know, those moments when the choice you're making feels so big, so true, that it's almost like it's coming from outside of you.

"But it's not. It's just you. Making the right choice, the only choice. So you never have to regret what happens next, no matter how things shake out."

I squeeze his hand. "I love you."

"I love you, too," he says. "And as long as we're acting from that place, I choose to believe that everything is going to be okay."

I tilt my chin, glancing up to see him glowing in the setting sun, his long lashes and the hint of stubble on his chin shining white gold, making him look more like an angel come to spread the good news than a man who's planning a murder. But that's because he's telling the truth, we *are* acting from a place of love.

Love for each other and for people whose goodness and innocence make them easy targets for the predators of the world.

"You know what I've been thinking?" I whisper, still soaking in the beauty of him, wanting to remember the way he looks right now for the rest of my life.

"What?" His gaze is still fixed on the horizon, where the day is rapidly slipping away. The sun is running toward the other side of the world where other people are sitting on other beaches waiting for it to rise, waiting for that eternal sign that there is light at the end of the darkness.

"Maybe we're all monsters." I turn my gaze back to the sea. "But we can choose what kind of monster we want to be. The kind that tears other people apart or the kind that fights to protect the things we love."

He grunts. "I don't think we're all monsters. Only the best and the worst of us. The rest are too lazy to care this much."

I smile. "You're pretty smart for a guy who graduated with a C average."

"I do my best," he says with a soft laugh. "Have to at least try to keep up with you."

"You do more than keep up with me. You make me better."

"Ditto." He brings our joined hands to his mouth, pressing his lips to the back of my hand.

We sit in silence as the wavy red yolk of the sun slithers into the sea. The sand begins to cool and the pink light fades to a moody blue, but still we sit side by side, saying goodbye to who we were.

But it's not a sad goodbye.

The past is full of beautiful ghosts, but it's haunted by uglier things, too. I'm ready to move forward, to make this choice and never look back.

Danny

On Sunday, we finalize our plans, gather materials and get everything in place for Tuesday night. On Monday, we hike into the jungle with the rest of the guides and the friends they've brought along as guinea pigs for their last training exercise, an overnight trip we'll spend camping on a sheer rock face.

Tonight was the night I'd planned to take care of the Sigma Beta Epsilon brothers when I thought I would be taking on all four of them alone. Instead, I'm here with Sam, and in roughly thirty-six hours we'll be back on track to the life we almost lost.

We reach the entrance to the canyon by noon and by two o'clock we've reached the base of the three hundred meter cliff where we'll be spending the night. Paola and the other guides take point on getting their friends ready for the climb. I shadow them, making sure they remember everything we worked on and then head back to Sam, who greets me with that new, serene smile of hers.

As I check her harness, making sure to cop a feel while I do, she laughs and swats me on the ass.

Ever since our talk on the beach, we've both been strangely calm.

Or maybe not so strangely.

Sometimes, the build up to a hard decision is the worst part. Once you've made up your mind, the stress fades away. I'm sure it will return tomorrow night when our decisions become actions, but for now, we're at peace.

The climb is intense, but amazing, granting ever more magnificent views as we creep above the tree line and the jungle stretches out beneath us. By five o'clock, we're two hundred meters in the air, setting up our ledges and tents and preparing to cook the stew we brought over tiny propane stoves.

Sam and I set up the tent we'll share on my ledge, but we leave hers bare. After our dinner is warmed, we sit on the edge of the clear platform with our legs hanging over the vast emptiness, watching the birds darting in and out of the canopy below like dolphins jumping out of ocean waves.

From our right and left come the soft conversations of friends, Ram and his brother arguing over what kind of meat is in the stew, Paola and her girlfriend laughing about their last camping trip and the monkeys who stole their breakfast, forcing them to hike home hungry the next day.

When we're finished with our stew, I toss around the bag of chocolate covered coffee beans I brought as a treat. We laugh as we chuck the paper bag from platform to platform, cussing Ram's brother when he nearly drops it over the edge. While the chocolate melts on our tongues, we talk about all the places we've worked, where we'd like to go next, and our adventure bucket lists. Paola wants to go to Iceland, Ram has a ticket to Fiji and will be leaving next August, and Sam tells them we're on our way to Thailand for a non-working vacation before we head home.

It's a beautiful night shared with good people and when Sam and I crawl into our tent not long after night-fall, I feel grateful. If, God forbid, something goes horribly wrong tomorrow, we couldn't have asked for a better last night of freedom.

We tie back the flaps to the tent so we can see the stars from our sleeping bag and hold hands in the dark, listening to the getting-ready-for-sleep sounds coming from the other tents. And when the teeth brushing is finished and the call of nature answered—a discreet whizz over the edge of the ledge for the men and bottles filled in the tent and dumped over the side for the women—and everyone else is finally asleep, it's so quiet it feels like there's no one else alive in the world.

No one but Sam and me, happily marooned on this tent pitched at the edge of nowhere.

"Where is home now, do you think?" she whispers, her voice husky in the darkness.

"Wherever we are. Together." I swear I can hear her smile.

"Where are we going to be together? I haven't wanted to think about it until this was finished, but after hearing everyone's plans I started wondering where we'll end up. And what I'll do when we get there."

"I could hire you on as my business manager in Croatia." I curl my arm around her waist. "I can't pay much, but benefits include housing, food, and unlimited oral sex privileges."

She laughs softly. "Giving or receiving?"

"Both. I'm a generous employer."

"Very generous," she says, fingers trailing back and forth across my chest, making me wish I'd taken my tee shirt off so I could feel her touch on my bare skin. "I'm sure my stepmom would help me find a job on Maui, but I don't know if I'm ready to go back there. I don't know what I'm going to say to them after disappearing for so long."

My smile fades. "I think you were right before. Let's cross those bridges when we come to them. No point in borrowing worries from the future when there are plenty here to go around."

"Are you worried?" she asks, her palm coming to rest above my heart, which beats slow and steady.

"No. Just...focused. The future isn't pushing on me the way it does sometimes. I guess it feels like it will take care of itself."

"Or it's already taken care of itself," she says. "You know Einstein said the separation between the past, present, and future is an illusion. Although a very convincing one."

I think on that for a moment, staring up at the night sky, seeing the light that left those stars thousands of years ago. Some of the lights twinkling in the darkness, seeming so set in their place in the sky, might be dead already. I'm not seeing what is but what was, a long, long time ago. It's all a matter of perception.

So maybe the future is the same way.

Maybe it's already there, written out on a page I can't see from where I am now. Or maybe it's waiting on what I'll do next, the letters trembling as they prepare for the present to mold the story they will tell.

"So if the separation is an illusion and they're all existing at once," I ask, brow furrowing. "Does that mean that the past could be as changeable as the future?"

"That's a nice idea," she says, her fingers resuming their hypnotic brush back and forth across my chest. "Or a scary one, I guess. Depending on how you look at it. What if I changed the past and never met you?"

The possibility bounces off of my mind without making an impression. Maybe before I spotted Sam in the airport, it would have scared me, but now I know better than to think anything can keep us apart. "Would never happen. I've seen my past, present, and future. You're in all of them. If there's one thing I know for sure, it's that."

She leans in, kissing my cheek. "Romantic."

"Guilty." I turn, finding her lips in the dark and giving her a proper kiss, the kind of kiss a woman deserves on a night like tonight.

My hand drifts from her waist to her breast, my thumb brushing over her nipple through the fabric of her sports bra.

"We shouldn't," she whispers even as she shifts, granting me better access.

"We should," I say. "We will."

It isn't easy getting out of our clothes with the harnesses still in place, but we manage, hands quiet and clever because they know our future holds pleasure. Not being able to see her makes her skin feel even softer, making me hyper-aware of each dip and hollow, each lovely curve and irresistible inch of slick, wet flesh.

So sweet. She is so sweet.

I bury my tongue inside her and taste eternity. Time stands still and there is only this, only us. Only her fingers tangled in my hair and her thighs trembling on either side of my face and her breath whispering in the dark. It comes faster, deeper, and then she comes with a tiny whimper, careful not to make a sound the others can hear. But I know she's tumbling over, I can taste it in the clean, salty rush of wetness on my tongue, feel it in the way her pussy plumps beneath my mouth, like fruit, full and heavy, ready to fall from the tree.

I move over her, kissing her with the taste of her still in my mouth, wanting her to know how sweet she is. Our tongues dance as her legs wrap around my waist, drawing me in to her.

This time, there is no fumbling in the dark. My body knows where to go. It has always known because I was born to make love to this woman.

I sink into her with one long stroke, her body pulsing around my cock as I bury myself inside her heat, her love. I hold her closer and rock into her, every thrust a promise that this is unshakable, this is what she can count on when everything else is chaos and insanity.

This is past, present, and future. This is truth. This is everything.

The climb is slow, steady, spiraling higher and higher until the air feels too thin and there's nothing to breathe but Sam. But she is enough, more than enough. We keep climbing, clinging to each other, grinding closer, deeper, until the pleasure is painful and my entire body screams with the need for release.

And then Sam lifts into me, her orgasm demanding my own, and takes the pain away and there is only pleasure so pure and perfect there is no room for anything else.

I come without a sound, not wanting to share this with anyone who might still be awake and listening.

This is only for us, for me and Sam.

"Let's get married," I whisper as we lie fused together, catching our breath.

"I thought you didn't want to think about the future." She wraps her legs around my waist, holding me inside of her.

"That's not the future," I say. "That's here and now. You're mine and I'm yours. We just need to make it official."

"I am yours," she says with a happy sigh. "That was... so perfect. I love making love to you. I want to do it every day for the rest of my life." She sighs again. "Except on the first day of my period, when I'm not in the mood."

I laugh, pressing a kiss to her forehead. "Is that a yes?"

"Yes." She hugs me closer. "But I don't want a big deal. I just want it to be you and me in some place pretty. Maybe on a portaledge on a cliff somewhere and then the person who marries us can climb back down and we'll spend the night just like this."

"Sounds perfect."

We talk a little longer, daydreaming out loud the way we used to when we were younger, imagining all the things we'd do when we were grown up and could finally be together all the time. I never imagined our lives would end up the way they have, but I can't regret any of it right now, with Sam in my arms and her "yes" still ringing in my ears.

I don't remember falling asleep, but when I wake up the stars are fading from the sky and the pale pink dawn is creeping up from the other side of the world.

I lie watching the light consume the last of the night sky, holding Sam in my arms, hoping that, by this time tomorrow, all the darkness will be gone.

CHAPTER NINETEEN

Sam

*"There is strong shadow
where there is much light."*
-Goethe

When you've been waiting on something for a long, long time, and then the moment you've been anticipating is suddenly at hand, it can be hard to know what to feel. It's like the anticipation of the event has become its own separate entity, a thing that's hard to let go of.

I have a hard time letting go.

I wake up in a daze and stay there as we pack up camp and make our way back down the cliff.

Today is the day. Today is the day that I will have my revenge.

Today is the day that two men will suffer and one man will die and then I will get on a plane and fly away with nothing to anticipate but how nice it will be to live in a world without Todd Winslow in it.

All the way through the jungle, my thoughts are a record stuck in a single groove, repeating the same things over and over again. But it isn't until Danny and I have hugged everyone goodbye and are back in the cabin, packing up our things, that reality finally settles in.

The fear hits a moment later.

A moment after that, I'm on the floor with my head between my legs, hyperventilating, trying my best not to pass out.

"It's okay." Danny rubs my back in soothing circles. "It hit me about an hour ago. It will pass. Just give it a second. Think about right now and nothing else and you'll be okay."

I bring my thoughts to this moment, to the worn wooden floor beneath my feet and the lizard who slithered under the bed when I plunked down a little too close to him. I think about drawing breath into my body and letting it out and the faint smell of wood smoke and mildew that lingers in the cabin. I think about the crick in my neck from sleeping on the tiny camping pillow and the more pleasant ache between my legs from making love.

After a few more breaths, I lift my head and look at my half-filled backpack.

I need to finish packing. That's what I'm doing right now. I'm packing. I'm not drugging anyone or dumping them in a pit in the middle of the jungle. I'm not watching someone convulse as they die from a lethal dose of arsenic.

If I keep imagining what's going to happen, I'm going to live through it a hundred times before nightfall and I won't have any energy left for the actual event. When the time comes, I have to be strong, solid, and focused, not drained and freaking out. I've spent a year training my body to face the men who hurt me, but only now do I realize I should have been training my mind as well. I'm beginning to think that in order for a murder to go off without a hitch, the mind is the most important muscle involved.

Luckily, mine has Danny to help it stay on task.

After I'm finished packing, he hands me a dust rag and a broom and leaves me to start cleaning up the cabin while he runs out to the mess hall. By the time I'm finished dusting and sweeping, he's back with a loaf of bread, a jar of peanut butter, and a few oranges he's liberated from the kitchen and puts me to work making sack lunches for our dinner while he cleans the bathroom.

Because one shouldn't commit murder or kidnapping on an empty stomach.

The thought inspires a sharp, hysterical burst of laughter, but luckily Danny is flushing the toilet and doesn't hear me.

That's good. I don't want him to be worried about me. I'm ready for this and as long as I keep busy I'm not going to have a breakdown.

We leave the commune just after three o'clock, allegedly on our way to a romantic dinner in the next town over. The dinner is our excuse for begging off from a night on the town with Paola and the rest of the guides to celebrate our last night in Costa Rica.

As Danny drives, I let myself imagine what it would be like to be the Sam they think I am, a woman without a care in the world but what exotic location she and her boyfriend are on their way to next. I imagine that Sam, drinking beers by the beach with her new friends and then getting talked into dancing at the tiny club in town, wiggling to perky techno music that never seems to make it onto the airwaves in the states.

It's so real I can almost see it.

So real that I think maybe that Sam does exist somewhere, in a parallel universe where I wasn't shattered and put back together with sharper edges than I had before.

But her world isn't my world, and by the time we reach the rental house and park the car in the garage, I'm coming fully online for the first time all day. As Danny and I pull on our gloves—we're not going to leave any prints behind—and do a quick check of the house and the surrounding areas, ensuring the house across the street is still unoccupied and no one will be watching our guests pull in later tonight, my blood rushes faster and my senses sharpen. I feel like I used to right before a volleyball game in high school, after our coach had delivered the pep talk and we were just waiting to run out onto the court.

Everything is ready, now it's just a matter of sticking to the game plan and following through.

"I'm going to tell Rosa to text me if she has any trouble getting J.D. and Jeremy out of the hotel," Danny says after we've each forced down half a sandwich and some water. "If I don't hear from her within ten minutes of dropping her off, I'll be on my way back here. I'll text you before I head out."

I force myself to exhale slowly. "I'll be ready. Be careful."

"I will." He watches me for a beat, before he adds, "This is it. Last chance to bow out. I can handle it alone if you need me to."

I shake my head. "No. I'm nervous, but I want to be a part of it. I need to be a part of it."

"Okay." He squeezes my hand. "It's almost over. Just keep remembering that. It's almost behind us."

"Love you." I lean in for a kiss, which he returns, firmly, but sweetly, and then he's gone.

After he leaves, I change into my blacks in the garage and pull my hair back into a bun I'll tuck under my sock mask when the time comes. I scan the concrete for hairs and tuck the few I find into the pocket of my black jeans, determined not to leave any DNA evidence behind.

Last, I check the lock on the front door to make sure it's open, turn the radio on in the living room so it sounds like there's a party in the house, and get the ketamine injections ready to go.

It seems like only a few minutes have passed when Danny texts me that operation Rosa was a success and he's on his way back.

All day long, time has been dragging, but now everything speeds up until it feels like the future is a bullet train bearing down on me and there's no time to get off the tracks. But I don't want to jump to safety. I'm going to stand and face the future.

Because the past demands it.

Because on New Year's Eve a year and a half ago, four boys set this series of events in motion. They created the monster I am now, and tonight, they are going to reap what they have sown.

Ten minutes later, I hear the car pull into the garage and the garage door humming closed. A moment later, Danny hurries into the foyer, an aluminum baseball bat in one hand and our sock masks in the other. "They're not far behind me. We should get ready. Remember, most important thing is that we get the door closed behind them before we make a move."

I nod. "I'll take care of Rosa and then come help you if you need it."

"All right," he says, pulling the sock mask on, making his lips look fuller and pinker in contrast with the rough fabric covering the rest of his face. "But I think I'll be okay. They should be too stunned to fight back while I'm giving the injection. I just have to be sure not to hit them too hard."

I slip the mask over my face and tuck my hair underneath. When I open my eyes again, I'm seeing Danny through frames of black cotton and the reality of the moment hits hard enough to make me flinch.

It's here. We're ready and there is no turning back.

"See you on the other side," he says softly.

"On the other side."

He reaches out a hand and I take it, squeezing his fingers between mine, drawing strength from his touch, his presence. Tonight, I am not alone. Tonight I have the upper hand and J.D. and Jeremy are going to learn what it feels like to be powerless and terrified.

Outside, the sound of a car pulling into the driveway rumbles through the night air before it falls silent. A car door slams and a moment later, I hear Rosa's laugh and her lightly accented voice telling the men that the rest of the party is inside. My hand slips from Danny's as I move back into the shadows behind the door and he takes his place around the corner, hidden from view in the hall leading into the kitchen.

Any second, the men I came here to punish will be walking through the door.

The knowledge fills my mouth with a bitter, acrid taste. My heart races and my nerve endings feel like they're catching fire, but at the center of the storm, there is a calm place that fear and panic can't touch. And from that calm place I reach into my own mind, doing what I have to do.

I take a deep breath and let go, pulling back the calloused skin that protected me for so many months, flinging open mental doors I've learned to keep locked tight. These are the rooms where the horror lives, where there is nothing but blood and pain and the sounds of my own screams. But tonight, these memories won't bring me nightmares or leave me sweating and shaking in my bed, reliving every helpless moment until I don't know if I'll live to see morning.

Tonight, they will bring me strength.

As the doorknob begins to turn, time slows to a crawl and I go back.

Back to the pool table's rough felt beneath my cheek, back to the smell of sour beer and whiskey breath and the sweat of unfamiliar male bodies dripping onto my face. I go back to J.D.'s hands shoving me down onto the table and ripping my jeans down my legs while I kicked and screamed and Todd and Jeremy egged him on.

He was the first and I was still fighting hard. J.D. isn't

much taller than I am or much bigger. There was a chance I could have fought him off if Jeremy hadn't crawled up on the table and grabbed my wrists, pinning them to the felt as he trapped my head between his thighs and squeezed, holding me in a vice grip between his legs as J.D. forced himself inside me, tearing me apart.

I had never been with anyone but Danny, had never known any pain associated with sex except that slight sting and ache the night Danny and I were each other's first. He had always been careful with me, always taken the time to be sure I was ready.

J.D. didn't take time; he took my dignity.

He took something that should only ever be about pleasure and gave me pain and degradation. He showed me that I was nothing to him. I was not human or even animal. I was an object unworthy of kindness or compassion. I was something to be used to make him feel powerful and then passed around to his friends.

Now, he will pay.

Now, he and Jeremy will learn what it feels like to be nothing.

I watch Rosa swing inside, wearing a tiny red dress and stiletto heels, in slow motion. My blood is rushing so loud in my ears I can't make sense of what she's saying to J.D. and Jeremy or what they say in return. I don't feel like myself anymore. I am nothing but rage so huge that it feels like my soul is expanding past the confines of my body until it fills the room, shatters the windows, explodes into the night sky leaving a trail of fire behind.

And then Jeremy and J.D. come through the door and everything happens at once.

Danny comes out swinging and Jeremy falls almost immediately, the thunk of the bat connecting with his skull followed closely by the sound of his body crumpling to the floor. J.D. turns to run, but I've already kicked the door closed. In my peripheral vision, I see Danny's bat swinging through the air as I reach for Rosa. She's unsteady in her heels and falls into me as I wrap my arm around her neck and squeeze, applying pressure to her carotid arteries.

I've never used full force before—sparring on the mats at the gym we were taught to hold back to keep from knocking our partner unconscious—and I'm shocked at how quickly she goes limp in my arms.

It takes maybe seven, eight seconds at most and then I'm guiding her carefully to the floor. I take a moment to look up and see that J.D. and Jeremy are flat on their backs and Danny is already jabbing a needle into Jeremy's thigh, before turning back to Rosa. I inject her with a much smaller dose of ketamine as gently as I can, not wanting to cause her any more pain, even if she is unconscious, and then sit back on my heels. Danny finishes delivering J.D.'s injection and looks up, meeting my gaze across the bodies littering the floor.

We're both still for a moment, catching our breath, and then Danny reaches down, grabs the car keys from where they've fallen, and tosses them my way.

I catch them with a steady hand.

"I'll get these two into the trunk," he says. "You want to pull their car out of the driveway so I can get out?"

I nod, loving him even more for knowing I need to keep this all business. There's no time for a post-mortem about the events of tonight until after it's all over.

And maybe not even then.

Maybe this is one of those things that we'll put to bed and never speak of again, like the time I kissed another boy at a graduation party, or last summer when Danny got drunk and said hurtful things that could ruin us if we gave those memories too much air and sunlight.

Some things are meant to be locked away in the dark and starved of attention until they all but disappear.

But before we can lock them away, we have to see this through.

I stand. "I'll get Rosa taken care of and meet you at the site."

"All right," he says. "Do you need me to come back in and help you get her into the trunk?"

"Nope," I say. "She's light and it's better for you to go. We don't want those two waking up before you get out of town. I'll text you after I've dropped her off. If you don't hear from me in thirty minutes, start without me."

"I'm not starting without you," he says, kneeling and picking up J.D. with a soft grunt. "If there are people outside her apartment, leave her on the street somewhere and call 911 to let the cops know where she is. The emergency number is the same here as it is in the states."

"I'm not going to leave her unconscious on the street," I say, knowing what can happen to women who are left alone and defenseless even for a few minutes. "I'll get her inside her building, and into her apartment if I can figure out which is hers, and I'll get to you as fast as I can."

With a resigned sigh, Danny carries J.D. into the garage. I pull their rental car out to the street and head back inside. While Danny loads Jeremy into the trunk beside J.D., I hustle into the living room and turn off the music before grabbing the bleach spray we bought and mopping up the blood smeared across the floor near Jeremy's head. J.D. and Rosa didn't make a mess so all that's left to do is lock up and get Rosa loaded into the trunk.

As I walk back to the curb to fetch the car, Danny is already backing down the drive. He pulls out into the street and shifts gears, heading off into the night without any parting words out his open window.

I know he thinks I'm taking an unnecessary risk with Rosa, but I have to make sure she's safe.

My revenge will not claim any innocent lives. And Rosa is innocent, no matter what kind of life she's chosen to lead. No woman, virgin or whore or anything in between, deserves to have her autonomy taken away. Our bodies belong to us and they are all equally valuable and sacred. I've used Rosa, but I won't abuse her, or leave her vulnerable to anyone else's abuse.

Carefully, I carry her into the garage and tuck her into the trunk. She's breathing easy, but I make sure to lay her on her side. I read that some people can have trouble breathing after a ketamine injection and it's better to be safe than sorry. I leave the key in the drop box by the front door where the rental agreement said to leave it and get back in the car. No one will be by to check on the house until after checkout time at ten tomorrow morning, and no one will be able to say that Danny and I didn't spend the night here.

Everything is going so smoothly, better than I could have imagined.

I arrive at Rosa's apartment to find the street deserted except for a couple of bums digging through the trash at the end of the block. I pull the car up to the curb, cut the engine, and wait. It takes a good twenty minutes, but finally the homeless men turn the corner, and I make my move.

I pop the trunk and swing out into the warm night. I've removed my mask, but my black long-sleeved shirt and jeans are still too warm for the tropical climate. I'm sweating even before I lift Rosa out of the car. By the time I get us both up the steps and the apartment building's sticky front door unlocked, beads of perspiration are rolling down my face.

One lands on Rosa's cheek as I lay her on the stained couch in the lobby. She flinches before letting out a low moan.

Considering her size, she shouldn't be conscious for another hour or two at least, but apparently Rosa has one hell of a metabolism and is already burning through the meds like a champ. She moans again and I launch into motion.

Heart pounding, I quickly wipe the sweat from her cheek with my sleeve, place her keys into her curled fingers, and head for the door. I force myself to walk to the car, knowing that running attracts attention. But I shouldn't have worried. There is no one to see me run, and no one to watch as I get back into the car and pull away.

I make it through town without incident, shooting

Danny a text that I'm on my way while stopped at a light near the central market.

His response comes through a second later. *See you soon, doll.*

Doll. The unexpected pet name makes me frown.

I'm a lot smaller than Danny, but after carrying another woman up a flight of stairs I'm not feeling delicate or doll-like. It bothers me for another reason, too. I'm not sure what it is, but I eventually dismiss the gnawing at the back of my brain, knowing I need to stay focused on more important things.

By the time I reach the gravel road and turn right, heading up into an isolated stretch of jungle not far from the airstrip where I brought Danny for target practice, I'm feeling pretty confident. If the second half of the night goes as smoothly as the first, we'll be at the airport early enough to grab breakfast in the terminal before we board our flight to Samui, Thailand.

I'm confident, but not cocky.

I've never been cocky, even back before the attack, when I was an athlete who had never met a ball she couldn't spike or a wave she couldn't ride.

I've always known that I have my faults and weaknesses. I've always been honest with myself, and I believe that honesty made me better.

While my teammates in high school were busy blaming a lost game on someone else's performance, I was watching video of the match and seeing where I could improve. When other surfers said they needed a different board or cleaner waves, I kept paddling back out until I found a way to work with whatever the ocean was giving me on a particular day.

I don't suffer from hubris, that overabundance of pride that doomed so many Greek heroes to tragic fates. I don't fly too close to the sun, I don't believe I can take on a six-headed sea monster and come out on top.

So when I pull into the clearing, where the hole Danny and I dug in the forest floor is waiting, to see the rental car's trunk open, the driver's door ajar, and the headlights casting eerie shadows across the mouth of the pit, I don't assume there is a reasonable explanation. I park near the trees, a good hundred feet from the other car and make as little noise as possible getting out. I can't see if J.D. and Jeremy are in the trunk or the pit, but there is no sign of Danny anywhere nearby and the jungle is weirdly quiet.

I resist the urge to call his name, not wanting to let anyone know I'm here if they haven't heard the car pull up.

Ears straining and my skin crawling with the certainty that something has gone horribly wrong, I reach into the backseat, open my backpack, and pull out the rifle. Danny wanted me to leave it buried in the woods behind the cabin, but I refused to get rid of it until after all our affairs were in order. Now, it gives me comfort to have a weapon, still assembled and ready to use.

Scanning the clearing, I don't see anyone watching me, but I can't know for sure. Still, it seems like a good idea to check the car. Hunching over at the waist, I creep slowly through the shadows, feeling exposed until I'm squatting down beside the open door.

A quick glance inside reveals nothing that would make me worry.

The keys are in the driver's seat, but Danny might have left them there, knowing no one would be around to snatch them. I look into the backseat, seeing his bat lying on the floor. But that still doesn't mean anything. With J.D. and Jeremy drugged, he probably wouldn't have thought he needed it.

Still...

I tuck the gun in the back of my jeans—grateful for its compact size—and reach behind the seats to grab the bat. We're a good three miles from the road, far enough no one will hear J.D. and Jeremy scream, but maybe not so far that the sound of a gunshot wouldn't carry. Just in case, the bat is a better weapon if I can get away with it.

Gripping the cool aluminum tight, I circle around to the open trunk and peek inside. J.D. and Jeremy aren't there. I'm guessing that means they're in the pit, but for some reason I'm scared to go look. I'm suddenly possessed by the unreasonable fear that if I stand at the edge someone will push me in.

Or maybe it's not such an unreasonable fear.

There's a chance the brothers have escaped. They might have woken up too fast, like Rosa, caught Danny by surprise, and beaten him unconscious before heading back to civilization. He might be out there in the jungle, bleeding to death under a tree somewhere, and if so, I can blame myself for it.

Blame myself, and my need for vengeance.

There was a choice to be made, like Danny said, and I've made the wrong one. I should never have put him in danger. I should have kidnapped him if I had to and made him run away with me. Only now, as I realize revenge might cost me the man I love, do I realize that it isn't worth it.

Yes, these men deserve to be punished, but love is more important. It's more important than the law that insists the brothers' fates belong in the hands of the court, but it's also more important than vengeance. It is bigger than this, bigger than the hurt and the pain and the hate. I feel that truth shudder through my bones as I start back toward the darkness at the edge of the clearing.

Slowly, squeezing the bat hard enough to make my knuckles ache, I creep around the perimeter of the bare earth with the pit at its center, keeping close to the trees, scanning the area for any sign of life. I move quietly, carefully, the bat cocked over my shoulder, ready to strike the second I have a target. I check the clearing and the shadows beneath the trees, just in case there is someone hiding in the woods.

Every sense in my body is on high alert, my ears straining for any sound that can't be explained away by the wind or some night creature stirring in the brush. I am so focused that I would swear I hear the almost inaudible hum of the bug lanterns before I see them. And I certainly see the lanterns—and the scene they illuminate—long before Todd sees me, but it doesn't matter.

And it doesn't matter that I know I could take Todd out with this bat if I had to, not when Todd has a knife pressed to Danny's throat.

CHAPTER TWENTY

Danny

"Choose well.
Your choice is brief,
And yet endless."
-Goethe

I try to call out to Sam, but Todd wedges the knife tighter to my throat, transforming my words into a guttural cry.

He's going to kill me.

I knew it the moment he stepped up behind me at the edge of the pit and pressed the knife into my back hard enough to rip a hole through my shirt and break the skin. I'm not leaving Costa Rica alive, but Sam still can, if I can just get the words out. I have to tell her to run, to get to the car and drive away as fast as she can.

I chose this. I knew there were risks, but I made this

choice anyway. I hope she won't blame herself or doubt that I love her as much as I ever did.

Because I do. So much.

Even after I'm gone.

I can handle dying as long as I know she's okay. But I can't go out knowing she's alone in the jungle with Todd, that I've failed to protect her, and he's going to hurt her all over again.

"Put the bat down, doll," he says. "Or I start cutting off pieces of your boyfriend."

"I'm not your doll." Sam's breath rushes out, but she doesn't drop the bat. She takes a step closer to the stump where Todd has me seated in front of him, with my body shielding his and his knife pressed to my throat.

Even if he let me go, there's no way I could run. My legs are bound and my arms tied in front of me from wrists to elbows with my own rope. I had just finished tying J.D. and Jeremy's arms together and rolled them into the pit when Todd came out of nowhere. I didn't hear a car engine or footsteps or anything. He just materialized out of thin air, like an evil genie, come to prevent wishes from coming true.

"Do it now," Todd says again, still in that calm voice that makes it clear he knows he's won. "You know I don't bluff. You take one more step with that bat and he loses an ear. I saw the dents in Jeremy's head. I don't need a matching set."

Sam stops, swaying on her feet for a moment before she crouches down, laying the bat in the dirt. "There. It's down. Now let him go."

Todd chuckles. "Take five steps to your right and sit down against that tree."

Sam's eyes meet mine and I shake my head. The movement ends in a groan as Todd's knife slices the skin at my throat, but it will be worth it if Sam will run.

Please, Sam, I beg with my eyes. *Please, run. Run!*

"Stop," she says, voice breaking. "Don't hurt him. I'm going."

"Run," I gasp. "Run!"

Todd silences me by wrapping his free hand around my neck and squeezing until the world goes black around the edges. I buck against his hold, but in this position I can't get any leverage. All I can do is arch my back, flex the muscles in my throat, and fight to keep him from crushing my windpipe. I fight back as best I can, but by the time he releases me, I'm dizzy and weak, with black spots dancing in front of my eyes and blood thudding heavily in my ears.

"Next time you talk, you die," he whispers into my ear, his lips moving against the sweat-slicked skin of my cheek, making me shudder.

His whisper is more convincing than a scream.

He isn't making a threat to scare Sam. Sam probably couldn't even hear him. He was making me a promise, one I know he'll keep if I open my mouth again.

Swallowing hard, I look up to find Sam seated against the tree, her legs drawn to her chest. She's in an upright fetal position, arms clenched tight around her legs, but I can still see her shaking. Her entire body seems to vibrate, making the curls that have escaped her bun dance around her head. Her eyes are wide and she looks terrified, but I know her better than that.

Sam doesn't shake like that when she's scared.

She only shakes that hard when she's angry.

I try to take comfort in the fact that she's going to fight back, but I'm too damned sick to my stomach. I don't want to die like this. I don't want her to be forced to watch. And I sure as hell don't want her to die.

I want to marry her on a beach in Thailand. I want to take her home to Croatia and celebrate with my family. I want to watch her hair grow out to its old beautiful brown with the red streaks in it and the joy return to her eyes. I want the happiness and the time and the love and the children and the *life* that this monster and his friends have done their best to ruin.

I don't want evil to win another round and steal all of it away before our second chance has even gotten started.

"So what happens next?" Sam asks, her voice rough with emotion. "What do you want?"

"I want to show you what happens to people who fuck with me and my friends," Todd says, then adds with a laugh, "I'm kidding. I don't give a shit about Scott ending up in jail or J.D. and Jeremy being buried alive. Or whatever it was you had planned back there with that hole in the ground. People stupid enough to drop their guard deserve what they get.

"But I know I would have been next, Sammy, and that isn't okay." He pauses, teasing the knife up and down my throat. "How did you plan to do it? Strangle me in my bed after you were finished filling in that hole?"

"Poison," Sam says flatly. "We were going to bribe a

maid to bring you a nightcap, then break into your room and watch you die."

Todd makes a considering noise. "Not a bad plan, but poison is kind of a girly choice, don't you think? Weak, especially for a big guy like you, Daniel Cooney."

He reaches around, hitting me in the stomach hard enough to make me groan and leaving his fist pressed tight to my gut, making it hurt to breathe. "I thought you looked familiar that day at the pool, but when I saw you the second time everything clicked. That's when I knew I had to start watching my back, and the other idiots, too. I figured you were responsible for poor, dumb Scott and that the rest of us must be on your hit list."

The fist he's digging into my mid-section relaxes, his fingers uncurling until his palm rests lightly on my abdomen.

But his touch is no less terrifying in its gentleness.

If anything, the brief break in the cruelty is worse, the knowledge that the reprieve won't last for long making my aching stomach feel like it's turning inside out.

"When I saw Jeremy and J.D. heading for the parking lot with that hot little thing in the red dress, I knew Danny had something to do with it." His hand moves in a circle, caressing my gurgling belly, making me shudder. "They don't have the creativity to convince a girl to fuck them both at the same time, no matter how much they've been wanting an excuse to get their cocks out in the same room again. So I followed them and then I followed you, Danny. I didn't realize you were here too, Sam, until you came out of the house, but I'm not surprised. You two have done everything together, haven't you? Since you were kids?"

Sam doesn't offer an answer, but Todd obviously doesn't need one. He's perfectly happy listening to the sound of his own voice.

He turns to me and sighs, the feel of his breath hot on my neck sending a fresh wave of dread shivering across my skin. "And now here we all are, ready to learn some important lessons from each other. I am going to learn never to leave someone alive who should be dead, and you are going to learn how stupid you were to fuck with someone meaner and smarter than you are."

Sam claps her hands together, slowly and deliberately, drawing Todd's attention back to her. "That's a real hero story, Todd. So you're the big winner. What are you going to do now, go rape some girls in Disney World?"

The knife leaves my neck, but Todd's hand replaces it, squeezing tight. "No, Sam. I was thinking, since you and Danny love to share experiences so much, that I'd fuck his ass while you watch. That sounds like fun, doesn't it?"

I have time to see Sam's face go white and then Todd's palm hits hard between my shoulder blades.

With my arms and legs bound, I can't keep my balance. I fall forward, my face in the dirt and my ass in the air.

Bile pushing up my throat, I try to crawl away, but Todd is already behind me, cutting through the waistband of my jeans. There is an ugly ripping sound as the fabric gives beneath his jerking hands and then my boxers are down around my thighs and Todd's knife is pressing into my stomach.

"Don't take a step away from that tree," Todd barks. "You do and his intestines will be on the ground before you can take another one."

"Please don't," Sam begs. "Please don't hurt him. Please!"

"But hurting's the fun part."

I feel him tugging at his clothes behind me and then his erection bobs free, falling heavy and thick against my ass cheek, and it feels so wrong I can't control my response.

I lurch forward, instinctively trying to escape, but he tilts the blade, jabbing it into the thin skin below my navel, piercing the skin, summoning a stream of blood that rushes down my thigh.

White-hot pain follows a second later, making me scream.

The pain is bad enough to stop me cold and suddenly I am aware of a hundred things all at once.

I'm aware of the breeze stirring my hair, of the heavy leaves slapping against the trunk of the tree, of Sam's tortured cry as Todd adjusts himself behind me, and the moans coming from the pit as J.D. and Jeremy begin to wake up. I'm aware of the blood coursing through my veins and the terror screaming in my head and a softer voice deep inside that insists I can survive this.

I can survive and when it's over, Todd's guard will be down.

Not even a monster can fight back in the middle of coming his brains out.

I grit my teeth and plan what happens next. I imagine the way I'm going to wait until he reaches the end and then hurl my body backward, pushing with my legs until he's pinned to the dirt with the air knocked out of him. Maybe the knife will fly out of his hand. But even if he keeps it, that moment of surprise will be enough for Sam to turn the tables on him. By the time I roll away, she'll have the baseball bat in her hands, beating the shit out of him.

I know it will happen. I can see it as clearly as I can see anything.

It's as clear as my memories of making love to Sam last night under the stars, of the way she looks running out of the ocean with her hair slicked back and her cheeks pink from the sun, of the way she smiled at me the day I told her I loved her for the first time. I was only a kid, but I knew then that I would do anything for her.

I would do anything.

Anything.

As Todd spreads my cheeks and puts the head of his cock against me, I know it's going to hurt, but the worst part is knowing that Sam is watching, and hearing her sob like her heart is breaking. I know if I let myself, I could cry with her. I could break down and sob like I haven't sobbed since I was twelve years old, wondering if my sister was going to be killed by the man who had abducted her.

But I'm not going to cry. I can't.

Not if I want to be ready.

And I'm going to be ready. He's not going to get away with this. He's not going to walk away this time.

He begins to push forward and I fight my own instincts, forcing myself to relax, knowing it will hurt so much more if I fight, knowing that I can't afford to be hurt that bad if I'm going to make him pay. But just before he breaches the tight ring of my ass, thunder booms through the clearing and his knife falls away from my stomach.

A second later, the pressure of his cock is gone and I hear a heavy thud as his body tumbles to the ground behind me.

Before I can fully comprehend that it's over or that the sound I heard wasn't thunder, but a gunshot, Sam is by my side, helping me up and pulling me into her arms. As I lean into her, I look down at the ground to see Todd's lifeless eyes staring up at the sky, a bullet hole through the center of his forehead.

"I'm sorry, I'm sorry, I'm sorry," Sam chants, her hands running over my body as if she can banish all the ugliness with her touch.

And she can. She will.

"Don't be sorry," I say, trying not to shake as I lift my arms between us. "Just untie me. And we'll finish this."

"I'm sorry," she says again, sobbing as she tugs at the knots holding my hands together. "I had to wait until he wasn't looking at me. I had to be sure I could get the shot in before he cut you again."

"It's okay." I roll my wrists, bringing sensation back into my fingers before reaching back to tug my boxers back up around my hips. But the movement makes Sam sob again and I wish I'd waited.

"I'm fine," I insist, shifting until I can sit and take her hands in mine. I wait until she looks up at me, tears spilling from her big blue eyes. The lantern light isn't that bright, but I can see how much she's hurting, how much she blames herself, and I refuse to let that happen.

"Please don't hate me," she whispers.

I don't say a word. I cup her face in my hands, pull her close, and take away her pain.

I consume her tears, kissing them away with my lips and tongue, taking all of her sadness into myself because I can handle it. I can handle it because she saved me from the nightmare she lived through. She saved me and there is no reason for her to cry for something that didn't happen.

Finally, her tears stop and my lips find hers and we kiss. And it is sweet and intense and filled with gratitude. It is all I wanted in those moments when I thought I was going to die. By the time we pull apart, tears are rolling down my cheeks, but they aren't sad tears.

I'm just so damned grateful.

"Don't be sad," I say, blinking fast, determined to pull myself together. "I love you. I don't blame you. Even if it had happened, I wouldn't have blamed you. You are mine and I could never hate you. No matter what."

"I love you," she says, brushing the tears from my cheeks with tender hands. "I don't ever want to see you in danger again. Promise me, never again."

"I can't promise that," I say. "Because the world is a shitty place full of terrible people, but I promise I'll always have your back. And I'll know I'm a lucky bastard that you have mine."

She leans in, hugging me tight for a long moment before she kisses my cheek and reaches down to untie the ropes binding my calves together. "Let's get out of here."

"The sooner, the better." Once I'm free, we grab Todd's knife from where it fell to the ground and hurry back to the cars, circling around the pit where either Jeremy or J.D. is moaning. We start our car, breathing twin sighs of relief when it turns over easily, the battery not drained by the time spent with the lights on.

Pulling out my pack, I shove my ruined jeans inside and grab a pair of shorts, tugging them on before taking the gun from Sam and wiping it down, getting all her prints off, while she takes a bleach rag to the bat and the knife. After, I wrap the gun and the bat together in the plastic from the trunk.

While she wipes down J.D.'s rental car, I take one of the lanterns and follow the trail back into the jungle to the second hole we dug the day we spent sweating in the sun with our shovels. I bury the weapons quickly and then cover the freshly turned earth with leaves.

If the police have dogs, there's a chance everything will be found, but there will be no prints and no way to track the illegally purchased firearm, Todd's knife, or a bat purchased with cash to either Sam or me. This is just a precaution, but one I'm glad we thought to take. After nearly dying, I have no interest in ending up in prison facing a death penalty.

I grab the wicker basket containing the snakes I bought from the weird dude down the road from the compound, chilled by the sudden squirming inside, and hurry down the trail.

Back at the clearing, I find Sam standing in between the headlights, chewing on her thumb as she stares down at the pit.

"You ready?" I ask, setting the wicker basket carefully down in front of her.

"What about the blood?" she whispers. "Todd might

have your blood on his hands. And I know there's blood on the ground. I saw it drip from your stomach while he was...while he was getting ready to do it."

I put my arm around her shoulder and pull her in for a hug, holding her close while I think.

"Well," I finally say, keeping my voice low in case J.D. or Jeremy is alert enough to be listening. "We can go clean it up the best we can, but I've never been arrested or enlisted in the military. My DNA shouldn't be on record. As long as I keep it that way it should be fine."

"That's not good enough. I need to know you're safe." She pulls away, looking up at me. "Do you still have your lighter in your pack?"

I nod. "You want to burn him?"

"We can use the basket to get it going," she says. "It's so dry, it should burn well enough. And we don't need the body destroyed, just for the fire to burn the skin with the blood on it away."

"And I can dig up the place where I bled on the dirt and throw it farther out in the woods." I grab my lighter from my pack and press it into Sam's hands before reaching for the basket handles. "I'll empty this in the pit and meet you by the body."

She touches my wrists. "No. I... I don't want to. Not anymore. Just let the snakes loose in the woods."

"You sure?" I say. "You're not going to regret it later?"

She shakes her head. "No, I'm not. We'll leave those two in there with their hands tied and let them figure their own way out. They will, sooner or later, and eventually they'll learn what happened to Todd. I think altogether that's a strong enough message."

"Then I'll let these guys out and meet you there."

By the time I dump the snakes in a gulley and make it back to the place where I almost died, Sam's got Todd propped up against the tree stump and a bundle of sticks wedged into the crevices beneath his back and under his legs.

"I already threw the dirt with your blood on it out into the woods," she says. "We just need to get him ready."

We tear the basket apart and stuff the pieces around the body, not speaking until the moment comes to light it up. Then, we stand side by side, staring down into the flat, empty eyes of a dead monster.

I don't know about Sam, but when I look at him, I feel nothing.

Not hate, not fear, nothing but exhausted by what we've been through and sickened by the gore beginning to drip from the hole in his forehead.

He isn't a monster now; he's just dead tissue.

Whatever it was that made Todd the nightmare he was—his mind or his soul—is gone. I don't know where it's gone, but I don't feel any guilt about my part in its destruction. And if there is a hell, I know he's on his way there, to rot and roast with the rest of the wicked things.

"To the end of it," Sam whispers, flicking the lighter on.

"To the end of it."

She lights the wicker pieces and they go up fast, flaming hot long enough to catch the sticks and Todd's clothes on fire. We stay until he is engulfed in flames and the smell of human skin catching begins to overcome the smell of burning sticks and cotton and then we turn and walk away.

One of the men is calling out from the pit as we get into the car, but we don't answer his cries for help.

We get in, buckle up, and drive away, and we don't look back not even when we're safely strapped in on a plane taking us far, far away.

EPILOGUE

Danny

One Year Later

"All the knowledge I possess
everyone else can acquire,
but my heart is all my own."
-Goethe

hey say absence makes the heart grow fonder, and for a long time, I thought that was true.

Forced to be away from Sam so much while we were growing up, I loved her more every time our separation ended and I could finally hold her in my arms again.

But after a year of marriage and constant togetherness—working and playing and healing together—I know it wasn't absence making my heart grow fonder, it was just Sam. It's how things are when something is meant to be. I still love her more every day, treasuring the fact that I get to go to bed with her every night and wake up to her every morning.

And today, I got to marry her all over again, on a cliff beside the Croatian sea, with our family and friends all here to help us celebrate. They don't know this was our second wedding or that we eloped in Thailand a year ago, but we thought it was best to keep that our secret.

They wouldn't have understood the two of us making such a major decision after Sam had spent a year in seclusion. They wouldn't have understood that a love like ours doesn't need long to fix the things that are broken, or that we needed to be married, just in case we were ever asked to testify against each other in court.

We haven't told a soul what we did, and even when the news came out about Todd's murder, no one asked if we were in Costa Rica at the same time as the SBE brothers. Not the authorities and not our family though I would bet my hands that Caitlin and Gabe know. The way my sister hugged me, the day Sam and I showed up on her front porch with everything we owned in the bags at our feet, made it clear how worried she'd been.

And how happy she was to have us both home safe.

"That was so beautiful," Caitlin says now, dabbing at her face with a tissue as she wraps her free arm around my waist. "You guys just about broke my heart with the vows."

"We've had a long time to plan them," I say, looking over my sister's head to where Sam is talking to her parents by the railing at the edge of the cliff overlooking the ocean.

In a white, flapper style dress, with her chin-length brown curls wild around her face and flowers in her hair, she is stunning. But it isn't just the dress or the flowers; it's the way she smiles when she looks over to see me watching and starts toward me across the grass.

It's her Sam the Shark smile, the one so big and wide one of her meaner friends used to make fun of her for it. I've always loved that smile, but I love it even more now because it means she's whole again.

There are scars on her heart that will never heal, and both of us lost what little innocence we had left last summer. But scars remind us to be grateful for beautiful days without any pain in them and innocence is overrated.

Our younger, innocent selves loved purely, but not as fiercely or selflessly as we do now. Now we know that there is nothing more precious than this. We were stripped bare, brought low, and met each other in the darkness where there was nothing but our love to lead us back to the light.

And it was enough.

More than enough.

Now, there is nothing left to be afraid of.

Let the world bring its worst. We're ready because there is no end to a love like this. Whatever comes after this life, I will be with Sam and she will be with me. We're not two trees with a fused trunk anymore, we are one heart, for now and always.

"No more crying," Sam says, pulling Caitlin in for a hug. "If you don't stop, I'll start again and I wasn't smart enough to wear waterproof mascara."

Caitlin laughs as she pulls away to wipe her eyes.

"Okay. I'll stop. I'm just so happy for you both. No two people have ever deserved happiness more."

I reach for Sam, but she's already wrapping her arms around my waist, sensing what I need before I have the chance to ask, the way she does.

"I don't know about that," she says, "but we're certainly grateful for it."

"We are." I hug her closer. "And I'm going to be even more grateful after we have cake."

Caitlin rolls her eyes. "You and Juliet. She's been trying to get her little arms elbows deep in that cake since she laid eyes on it." She turns, scanning the crowd for her daughter, laughing when she sees the two-year-old dashing across the grass toward the cake with her daddy not far behind. "I'd better go give Gabe a break before she runs him ragged."

"Tell her we'll be right over to cut her a big piece," Sam says. "We don't want to keep our favorite tyrant waiting."

"She is a tyrant," Caitlin agrees affectionately. "Good thing she's cute."

"Crazy cute," Sam agrees, smiling as Caitlin runs across the grass to scoop Juliet up in her arms, blowing kisses against her daughter's cheek until Juliet giggles.

Sam has grown closer to all my family in the past year, but she and Juliet have a special bond. They are kindred spirits, strong girls who know what they want and aren't afraid to let the world know about it. Though Sam has more patience. Most of the time.

"You didn't tell her did you?" she asks, tilting her head to look up at me, the setting sun making her eyes sparkle, taking my breath away.

"You look like a movie star right now. I swear you do."

Her smile shifts to the right. "That means you didn't tell her."

"I figured it could wait," I say, kissing her forehead. "I don't want to ruin the day for her. She's going to be sad to see us leave, even if it is only for four months."

"I know." Sam lifts her chin, bringing her lips closer to mine. "But if we don't have our adventure now, we'll have to put it off for another twenty years."

"Not true," I say, kissing her, loving that she tastes like sunshine and happiness, exactly the way a bride should taste on her wedding day. "When they're teenagers, we could leave the kids with Caitlin and Gabe for a few months and sneak off. Teenagers suck anyway."

Sam smiles. "That's why they need parents around, to keep them from sucking. And I'm sure Caitlin and Gabe will be busy enough with their own obnoxious kids."

I bring my hand to her flat stomach, still finding it hard to believe our baby is in there, growing bigger every day. "I can't wait until I can feel her kick."

"Or him," Sam says. "It might be a boy, a boy as gorgeous and wonderful as his daddy."

I shake my head. "Trying to butter me up so you'll get laid tonight?"

"Oh, I'm getting laid tonight," she says, eyes narrowing as she grins. "I have a letter from the doctor saying it is completely fine for us to have sex. I went to her office this morning and made her write it out, even though she thought you were crazy for worrying."

"I'm not crazy," I say though I'm secretly relieved. It's been hell keeping my hands to myself the past week since we found out. Unexpectedly, knowing Sam is pregnant with our baby has given me a hard-on that won't quit.

"You are crazy," she says, hand drifting down to pat my ass. "But also very, very sweet."

"Are you fondling my ass in public?"

"Yes," she says, still grinning. "I'm allowed to do that now that everyone knows we're married. It's one of the perks. At least for the first year. Public butt fondling is forgiven if you're a newlywed."

I slide my hand around from her belly to her bottom, fighting to keep my body from responding too obviously to her closeness. "I didn't know that. I like that perk."

"I thought you might, but I—"

Sam doesn't get to finish her sentence before Juliet collides with our knees, wraps her chubby arms around our calves, and howls, "Cake, pease cake, pease cake!" in such a pitiful way you would think the kid hadn't been fed in a month.

"Yes, Jules, I'm so sorry," Sam says, scooping Juliet into her arms with a laugh. "It is past time for cake. Let's go get some. Right now."

"Yay! Cake!" Juliet's tears vanish, replaced by a big grin that makes her blue eyes sparkle just like Sam's.

I stay where I am for a minute, watching my wife carry my niece across the grass to the small tent where our wedding cake sits waiting to be cut. The way Sam holds Juliet so naturally, slung low on her hip with a hand cradling Jules' diaper-clad bottom, she looks like she was made to be an aunt, a mama.

She looks soft and sweet, but I know she is also a fighter and a survivor. I know she is as strong as she is tender and that I don't have to be afraid that life will break her again, not as long as we're together. And there is nothing I need in the world aside from that.

Aside from the one I love.

Halfway across the lawn overlooking the ocean, where the sun is setting slow, as if it hates to miss a moment of this perfect day, Sam stops and turns back to look at me and mouths, "I love you, too," like she knows what I was thinking.

And I'm sure she does.

Need more dark Cooney family romance?
Fall in love with Caitlin and Gabe's story in
A LOVE SO DANGEROUS.
Available Now.

Keep reading for a sneak peek!

SNEAK PEEK

Please enjoy this sneak peek of A LOVE SO
DANGEROUS, Caitlin and Gabe's story.
Available Now.

Gabe

The blonde dances like a woman possessed—arms up,
head tossing from side to side, hair flying, hips swiveling
with a sensual abandon that has the men surrounding
her twisting their necks to get a better look at her ass,
but she doesn't seem to realize she's causing a
commotion.

Or if she does, she doesn't care. She isn't dancing for
the people watching. This dance is about her and the
music. She's feeding off every pulse of the bass, every
eerie note the female singer croons about castles in the
sky. The girl dances like this moment is all there is, all
she needs, all she'll ever have, and I know right then—I
have to have her.

A second later I've dumped forty dollars on the table and I'm out of my booth, moving smoothly down the circular staircase to the dance floor, my double shot of whiskey forgotten. I ease off the last step and head straight for my girl, not surprised when the men and women in my way sense me coming and instinctively shift out of my path.

Over the past few months, I've stopped giving a shit about almost everything and I've started fearing nothing. One thing I've learned in that time is that average folks are scared of people like me. Humans are hard-wired to possess a certain degree of fear. Fear keeps us safe from predators. Fear keeps us out of the path of oncoming traffic and our fingers out of the flames. People who aren't afraid are dangerous, unpredictable, like a field full of landmines you're better off not trying to cross.

But I have a feeling my tiny dancer is the kind who enjoys danger.

I reach her as the bass line is escalating, thumping faster and faster, becoming a desperate, hungry pulse that fills the club and reverberates off the walls. Her hips keep time, wiggling in tight circles that make it impossible not to imagine her blond curls tumbling around her bare shoulders while she rides me, faster and faster until we both explode.

Judging by the expressions on the faces of the two meatheads in matching polos hovering behind her, the jocks were having similar thoughts, but when I move between them and the object of their desire, they step back. Their lizard brains can probably tell picking a fight with me wouldn't end well, even if my biceps aren't the size of watermelons.

Not sparing my competition another thought, I shift my focus to the girl's flying hair and undulating hips and let go. I let go of everything—the residual irritation from the time I wasted with Shannon, the burning in my gut from my latest fight with my parents, the heavy gray weight of the undeniable things I drag around behind me every minute of every day, and the frustrated ambitions that hover around me like a poisonous fog. It all vanishes, leaving nothing but the girl and me and the music.

I've been dancing less than a minute when she turns —pivoting toward me and moving in close—and I know she's felt it, the draw of two like-minded creatures, a pull a hundred times more powerful than the opposing poles of a magnet.

Some may say opposites attract, but when it comes to human nature, like craves like.

My girl shifts closer, so close the hair flying around her face lashes the bare skin below the sleeves of my tee shirt, leaving a pleasant stinging sensation behind. The smell of her—cedar and soap and darker, smokier things —fills my head, ratcheting up my awareness. It's an unexpectedly masculine smell, but I like it. It suits her, somehow. She might be smaller than almost every other girl on the dance floor, but her ferocity is evident in every hip swivel, in every confident thrust of her thin arms into the air.

By the time she fists her hand in my shirt, pulling me to her, I'm already halfway to being hard. Her curves pressing against me finishes the job, but she doesn't pull away when my erection brushes against her belly. In fact —from what I can see of her pink lips between the flashing lights and the hair swirling around her face—I think she smiles.

A suspicion of a smile is enough for me to wrap my arm around her waist and lift her slim frame, shifting my jean-clad thigh between her legs.

She stiffens slightly as I urge her closer, until every roll of our hips sends my thigh into intimate connection with her heat. Her fingers claw into my shoulders and I catch a glimpse of her full bottom lip trapped between adorably jagged teeth. She sighs and throws her head back, giving me a glimpse of her pale throat and a jaw so delicate I could fit it in one hand.

Her head snaps back up a moment later, her hair flying around both our faces, and I feel the last of her resistance vanish. She gives in to the moment, to the music, to the way our bodies fit so perfectly together it's as if God made us to dry hump on the dance floor of the only semi-cool club in northern South Carolina.

I pull her closer, driving my fingers through her hair as our foreheads touch. Her nails dig into my skin so hard I can feel it through my tee shirt, her breath is warm and sweet against my lips, and the soft sound she makes as I tighten my fist in her hair is enough to make my skin go fever hot all over.

I suddenly can't wait another minute to be alone with her. The music that was fuel for the fire is now a giant gnat buzzing around my head, keeping me from being able to hear the sexy little breaths my girl is making as our dance gets progressively more erotic.

"Let's go somewhere," I say in her ear—perfect seashell ear so sweet looking I can't wait to trace each curve with my tongue. "Get out of here."

She shakes her head as she pulls away, giving me my first good look at her face. "I can't, I..." Her words cut off, replaced by a shocked expression I'm sure mirrors my own.

And I don't shock easily. Not any more.

But finding out the wild, uninhibited stranger, who's been grinding on my leg in public, is the most uptight good girl I've ever met—a girl so good she nuclear bombed her entire life to enable her ghetto family's bull-shit—is shocking stuff.

Still, I recover before she does, and smile.

"Caitlin." I shout to be heard over the new song, a hip-hop number less pulsing than the techno number before it. "Haven't seen you in a while."

"You still haven't seen me," she says, swallowing hard. "This never happened."

I smile wider. "Oh, come on. You seemed to be enjoying yourself. I was. Sure you don't want to come back to my place?"

"No way in hell," she says, her mouth going tight around the edges, the way it did when she'd turn in her seat during study hall and demand that my friends and I shut up, because "some people need to get their home-work done before work, assholes."

Back then, she was so uptight it was easy to ignore how pretty she was, but now that I've seen her dance, smelled her intoxicating scent, and had her breasts flat-tened against my chest as she writhed against me, I don't want to ignore it. I don't want to let Caitlin walk away without finding out if there's more wild child hiding beneath her chilly exterior.

When she spins and hurries away without so much as a "fuck you," I follow, stalking her across the dance floor.

I'd never pursue a girl who legitimately had no interest, but I know Caitlin wants me, and I want to feel her fingernails digging into my shoulders again, this time with no clothes between us. I want to feel her breath hot on my lips as she calls my name when I make her come, and come, and come again, until neither of us can hold a thought in our heads and there is nothing in the world but how good it feels to fuck.

Hot, sticky, sweaty, no-holds-barred fucking until the sun rises tomorrow morning.

I have my share of addictions, but this is my drug of choice—the hunt, the rush as I see how fast I can get the woman of the night naked and willing. It usually doesn't take long. Ten minutes, fifteen—maybe an hour if she's one of those sweet, Southern types who still gives a shit if a guy thinks she's a "bad girl."

As far as I'm concerned, there is no such thing as a "bad girl," simply girls who've embraced their sexuality and refuse to feel shame about it, and those who haven't. But, if we *must* call women who like to come with a variety of consenting partners "bad girls," then I'm a fan.

Bad girls are one of my favorite things and—despite what I know of Caitlin's past—every second of that dance assured me she's my kind of woman. I'm the one pursuing her across the dance floor now, but I wouldn't be surprised to find myself handcuffed to her headboard by the end of the night.

In fact, I'd enjoy it.

A LOVE SO DANGEROUS is
Available Now.

ABOUT THE AUTHOR

Author of over forty novels, *USA Today* Bestseller Lili Valente writes everything from steamy suspense to laugh-out-loud romantic comedies. A die-hard romantic and optimist at heart, she can't resist a story where love wins big. Because love should always win.

When she's not writing, Lili enjoys adventuring with her two sons, climbing on rocks, swimming too far from shore, and asking "why" an incorrigible number of times per day. A former yoga teacher, actor, and dancer, she is also very bendy and good at pretending innocence when caught investigating off-limits places.

You can currently find Lili in the mid-South, valiantly trying to resist the lure of all the places left to explore.

Find Lili at www.lilivalente.com

Keep in touch with Lili...
Free book when you join Lili's newsletter
Friend Lili
Like Lili
Follow Lili on Bookbub
Follow Lili on Instagram

ALSO BY LILI VALENTE

Racy Royal Rom Coms

Royal Package

Prince of my Panties

Learn more here

Red HOT Laugh-out-Loud Rom Coms

The Bangover

Bang Theory

Banging The Enemy

The Rock Star's Baby Bargain

Learn more here

The Hunter Brothers

The Baby Maker

The Troublemaker

The Heartbreaker

The Panty Melter

Click here to learn more

The Bad Motherpuckers Series (Standalones)

Hot as Puck

Sexy Motherpucker

Puck-Aholic

Puck me Baby

Filthy Wicked Love

Crazy Beautiful Love

One More Shameless Night

Click here to learn more

Under His Command Series

(HOT novellas, must be read in order)

Controlling her Pleasure

Commanding her Trust

Claiming her Heart

Click here to learn more

To the Bone Series

(Sexy Romantic Suspense, must be read in order)

A Love so Dangerous

A Love so Deadly

A Love so Deep

Click here to learn more

Fight for You Series

(Emotional New Adult Romantic Suspense.

Must be read in order.)

Run with Me

Fight for You

Click here to learn more

Lover's Leap Series

A Naughty Little Christmas

The Bad Boy's Temptation

Click here to learn more

The Lonesome Point Series

(Sexy Cowboys written with Jessie Evans)

Leather and Lace

Saddles and Sin

Diamonds and Dust

12 Dates of Christmas

Glitter and Grit

Sunny with a Chance of True Love

Chaps and Chance

Ropes and Revenge

8 Second Angel

Click here to learn more

Co-written Standalones

The V Card (co-written with Lauren Blakely)

Falling for the Boss (co-written with Sylvia Pierce)

Click here to learn more

The Happy Cat Series

(co-written with Pippa Grant)

Hosed

Hammered

Hitched

Humbugged

Click here to learn more